ONE CHOICE I'D NEVER MAKE

A SWEET ROMANTIC COMEDY

NEVER SAY NEVER
BOOK FOUR

REMI CARRINGTON

Copyright ©2021 Pamela Humphrey
All Rights Reserved
Phrey Press
www.phreypress.com
www.remicarrington.com
First Edition

This is a work of fiction. Names, characters, businesses, places, events, and incidents are either the products of the author's imagination or used in a fictitious manner. Any resemblance to actual persons, living or dead, or actual events is purely coincidental.

All rights reserved. This book or any portion thereof may not be reproduced or used in any manner whatsoever without the express written permission of the publisher except for the use of brief quotations in a book review.

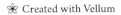 Created with Vellum

One Choice I'd Never Make

Never Date a Guy When Your World is Falling Apart

Being an only child has its perks . . . and its disadvantages. My parents want the best for me. That I get. But they also want to dictate my life.

Not gonna happen.

They want me to move back home, but I like living three hours away. Then I meet the perfect guy.

He's another reason not to leave my small town.

My parents don't like that I'm not moving—they don't know about the guy—and demand their stuff back . . . everything they've bought me. What am I supposed to do underemployed and without a car? I can't ask my boyfriend to save me from that.

But I'll do anything to figure out life on my own terms. Even if it means working on a goat farm.Once I establish my independence, I introduce Harper to my parents. They hate every choice I make, but I think they'll love him.

I'm not sure what I'll do if they don't.

CHAPTER 1

The downtown streets were quieter than they'd been three hours ago. I hadn't passed a single person in two blocks. Everyone else was probably tucked away in a fancy restaurant eating dinner.

The thought of dinner made my stomach growl. Why hadn't I brought along a change of clothes? I could've been enjoying dinner with friends instead of parading down the street like someone on their way to a Halloween party.

I glanced back over my shoulder and saw my tail lying on the ground. Stupid tail.

Keeping it attached to the back end of my costume was an exercise in frustration, so I shoved it into my oversized purse.

Back when I was in high school, my father had suggested I get a part-time job to develop a good work ethic. So, I did.

Bagging groceries seemed easy enough, but I was let go for being too friendly with the customers. Did they want me to walk around looking at the ground and grunting when asked a question? Apparently.

I stepped into the fast-food world after that. We weren't a good match. That was what every manager said.

After that, I ended up working in the mail room at my daddy's company. And I excelled. It wasn't hard. The envelopes had names on them. Cubicles had names on them. It was like a giant matching game.

My parents had laid out clear expectations for what I was supposed to do after high school. And I followed them... mostly. I went to a reputable university. I studied engineering. I graduated with honors and landed a job at a prestigious company.

That was where their plan for me and my plan for me diverged. I hated the job. Then I dated my boss because I thought it would make the job more exciting. That didn't work out. Being dumped during my lunch hour in my boss's office was exciting, but not in the way I'd hoped.

Then after flirting with his new assistant for weeks, the toad had the audacity to say he missed me and wanted to go out again. I quit.

That was the short version of how I'd ended up dressed in a cat costume in downtown San Antonio. Posing as a model paid actual money. And I needed that to eat. Running home to Mom and Daddy was not an option.

I'd do anything to avoid that. Well, maybe not anything. I never wanted to sever that relationship. I wanted them to be proud of me.

Quitting my engineering job already had me on thin ice. And displeasing Daddy was a choice carefully made. Call me spoiled, but I liked my creature comforts.

When he found out that I'd quit the engineering job, he'd suspended my fun money. Temporarily.

My phone rang, and I dug it out of my purse. "Hello?"

"Cami, are you sure you don't want to come to dinner

with us?" Nacha asked. "There's a group of us getting together."

"Nah, I didn't bring a change of clothes, and what I'm wearing isn't quite dinner attire." I hooked my purse on my shoulder and kept walking.

"Where did you park?"

"Not too far away. Up the stairs. To the left. Five stoplights to the right, then three stoplights left. Then down this alley-type thing. Near that big shiny new building."

She chuckled. "Are you almost there?"

"About halfway. Maybe." If I hurried, I could make it back to my car before dark. "Have fun. Bye."

It was one thing to be dressed in a leopard costume when the sun was still blazing in the sky, but after dark, it sent a different message.

And these high-heeled boots were not made for strolling down city streets. My choices were watching my steps to avoid breaking an ankle or watching my surroundings so I wasn't snagged off the street.

While I was fending off kidnappers with my x-ray vision, I missed the wad of gum on the sidewalk. I wrestled my boot free then dragged it on the concrete, leaving a faded pink smear behind me as I went.

I'd have to get some peanut butter to get it off my shoe. Or was that what they recommended for getting it out of hair? Either way, it was worth a try.

On Halloween when every teenager waited for the sun to disappear from view, it always took forever. But today, when I needed the sun, it dove toward the horizon like there was a prize for making it there before I reached my car.

I stopped and scraped my boot a time or two before walking again. Footsteps sounded behind me.

Speed-walking, I turned left. Had I passed five stoplights or only four? Definitely four. I turned right at the next light.

Three more lights and then the alley. If I could stay ahead of the creepy shadow, I could escape downtown with my life.

Even mostly broke, I liked my life.

The shadow rounded the corner, and I sped up a little more.

My heart thumped on my eardrums, making it hard to determine how close he was. I hung a left.

The parking lot was just through the little alley. I needed to make it through there, then I could run across the street to my car.

The footsteps sounded closer. Maybe they were just echoing off the walls. No one would see me in here if that shadow stalker grabbed me.

Another man appeared at the end of the alley, and he was headed straight toward me. As he drew closer, I noticed the firefighter logo on his T-shirt.

He had to be a good guy, right?

Hope so. I needed a superhero, and besides the shadow stalker, the firefighter was the only one around.

I broke into a run. He froze as I ran up and threw my arms around his neck.

"Please help me. There's a man following me."

His arms tightened around me. "It's so good to see you." He played the part perfectly.

"Thank you. You're my hero." My lips brushed his stubble, and I regretted trying to whisper in his ear.

He tensed.

Of course he did. A woman wearing a cat suit just threw herself at him. He probably thought I'd kissed his cheek.

Superhero guy didn't let go, and I didn't mind in the least.

All the romance novels I'd ever read talked about a tingle when fingers touched. My body felt like I'd stuck my finger in a wall socket.

I looked into his green eyes and swallowed. "Thank you."

"Ma'am, I've been trying to catch you. You dropped your jaguar tail." The voice didn't come from the man holding me. The shadow man had said that.

Was there room for me in the crack in the sidewalk?

After a deep breath, I stepped away from the hunky firefighter. "It's a leopard tail."

Later, I'd tell Nacha and Haley all about the muscles under his shirt. Right now, I needed to gather the last shreds of my pride and escape.

Shadow man was as old as my father but wasn't in great shape. It wasn't a wonder he hadn't caught me. The poor man was still trying to catch his breath.

Putting my escape plan into action, I stepped into the street. Running would seem undignified, so I marched—I was probably jaywalking—across the street, then climbed into my car.

The firefighter ran after me, but he had to wait for a bus to pass, so I was able to get moving before he ran into the parking lot.

When I looked in my rearview mirror, he waved.

Crap! My tail was in his hand.

CHAPTER 2

There were times when I'd had a bit too much to drink or way too much dessert, and I woke up the next morning with an overwhelming sense of regret. The worst time was when I didn't know the little cups of Jell-O were made with some sort of alcohol.

They tasted good, but I felt horrible the next morning. Seriously. When I wanted to know if they were just Jell-O, I shouldn't have asked the guy wearing the frat shirt who never strayed more than two feet from the keg.

In hindsight, I should've known.

Anyway, today, I woke up with regret. In my ongoing and unsuccessful hunt for a man, I'd stumbled on an ideal candidate. And what did I do?

I tucked tail and ran. No. I hadn't even thought to grab my tail. Now I couldn't even use the costume. But the worst part was that I left that gorgeous green-eyed hunk of a man standing on the sidewalk.

How many fire stations were there in San Antonio?

I entertained the thought for a few seconds before deciding I definitely shouldn't hunt him down.

To ease my regret—or replace it with a different type of regret—I decided to get doughnuts with my coffee on my way to work. That was one perk of living in the tiny apartment in the back of the photography studio. The little bakery right next door was like a second home. That was both good and bad.

I rolled out of bed, dodged the only comfortable chair in the room, then scooted past the small dresser stuffed with clothes. The rest of my wardrobe hung from a bar on the other side of the bed.

The whole room was definitely bigger than a postage stamp, but I'd seen taco trucks comparable in size. My belongings stacked in boxes contributed to the lack of space.

I pulled on a robe before trudging across the hall to the bathroom. With windows across the front of the studio, I never took chances. I was in the back, but still.

Staring at the mirror, I inhaled, ready to give myself a lecture. Self-talk, especially with eye contact, helped me remember what I should and shouldn't do when I was tempted to mix up those things on purpose.

I sighed. "Cami, don't hunt down the superhero. He thinks you're nuts."

Clearly the shadow man thought that because he said as much as I walked away. I think his actual words were "She's nuttier than a Mounds bar."

The joke was on him because Almond Joy's got nuts. Mounds don't.

Both had coconut in them. Did that count as nuts? I'd have to google it later.

A quick glance at the time kicked me into gear. Working the front desk in my pajamas wasn't allowed, and I still hadn't bought my doughnut.

I'd mastered the art of getting ready quickly.

Fully dressed and ready for work, I slipped out the front door and locked it behind me.

Right next door, the glorious pastries awaited me.

Waving at Tessa the owner, I pushed open the door and was greeted by the most fantastic aromas. "Tessa, I think this might be my favorite place in the whole wide world."

Delaney lifted her coffee cup. "I agree." She owned the lingerie shop in our little strip mall and came in almost every day.

Coming in here each morning was almost as much for the friendship as it was for the food and coffee.

Tessa, the best baker in the world, waved away the compliment. "It's just food." She settled the tab with a customer, then joined us at the end of the counter.

"No, my dear. What you bake is pure magic. And I need two doughnuts this morning." I hopped up onto one of the barstools. "And I should take a few photos and upload them to your page. Because your stuff looks as good as it tastes."

Delaney shook her head. "Uh-oh. Two doughnuts? What's wrong?"

Living the tail episode was embarrassing; telling it would be just as bad. "Remember how I mentioned I had a photoshoot where I had to dress up as a leopard? Well, when I was walking back to my car, there was a man following me."

Tessa gasped. "How scary."

"It was. Then I saw a guy in front of me on the sidewalk, and I'm not sure what I was thinking. My fear had me delirious. We were in an alley, and in the movies, horrible things happen in alleys."

Anyone who knew me knew that my crazy ideas had little to do with fear and more to do with impulse.

"Anyway, I threw my arms around him, hoping the man chasing me would think…" I shrugged. I could only hope it made sense to them in the way it had made sense to me.

Delaney nodded. "He'd think you weren't alone. Brilliant plan."

"The guy I hugged was a total hottie. Completely. But the other guy, the one chasing me, was only trying to give me back the tail to my costume. It had fallen out of my purse."

They both winced.

"Yep. So, I ran to my car. And now I need doughnuts because walking away from the hottie was maybe the dumbest thing I've ever done. And believe me, that says a lot."

Tessa leaned on the counter. "Did you even get his name?"

"Nope. Somewhere out there, a hot fireman has my leopard tail."

Tessa glanced up as the door opened. "What are you going to do?"

"Nothing. I'll probably never see that tail again. All I know is that my hero was wearing a T-shirt with a fireman's logo on it. Shoot, I'm not even sure he's single."

If he wasn't single, he needed to rethink how he hugged strangers.

"Are you going to the fire station after you have coffee?" Delaney laughed as she checked the time.

"He probably thinks I'm nuttier than a pecan-covered cheese ball." I made a mental note to buy one when I went to the grocery store.

"Maybe he likes cheeseballs." Tessa handed over two doughnuts, then went to wait on a customer.

"It doesn't matter because I'll probably never see him again." I sipped my coffee. "I'd love to chat longer, but I need to get to my desk."

"I need to run too. Inventory won't unpack itself and mannequins don't dress themselves." Delaney slid off her stool. "I like our morning chats."

"Me too." Tessa grinned. "A lot."

Moving to the small town had been unexpected but

helpful when I quit my engineering job. The longer I lived here, the more I loved it.

Mulling it all over in my head, somewhere between the doughnut shop and my desk, I decided not to breathe a word about my encounter with the hunky fireman to Nacha and Haley, my coworkers. Bosses would be a better description.

They rolled their eyes at my antics all the time. But today, I wasn't in the mood to deal with the head shaking and eye rolling... even if it was all meant in fun.

I carried the coffee and doughnuts to my desk and turned on the computer, getting ready for the day. While I liked working at the photography studio, the pay wasn't anything like my old job. And now that Daddy had cut off my fun money, I spent a lot of time considering the idea of another job. Since I didn't know what I wanted to do, it made searching a tad harder. And I liked working with Nacha and Haley.

Thinking about job stuff would only make today worse.

Haley ran in, her hair piled in a messy bun atop her head. "I'm so glad it's Friday."

"You and me both. Have you had a chance to look at the pictures from last night?"

She shook her head. "Nacha worked on those. What I saw on the camera looked good. You looked cute in your jaguar costume."

"It was a leopard costume." I think I was the only one who cared about the distinction.

"Whatever it was, you rocked it. I'm not brave enough to wear something like that, let alone walk around downtown in it."

"That's me. *Brave*." What a laugh. I was so brave I'd run into the arms of a stranger to save me from someone trying to return my tail. "I had fun though. I appreciate y'all giving me extra work like that."

"Always happy to do it. Well, I need to get to work. I'm hoping to slip out of here early. I want to go shopping at the little store down the way. Have you been in there?" Haley leaned out the door and pointed down the sidewalk.

"The lingerie shop? Delaney has super cute stuff, and that's the end of this conversation. I need to be able to work with you." I covered my ears for an added effect.

Haley rolled her eyes and walked back to her office, laughing.

Her timing was perfect because as soon as her door closed, the phone rang.

I answered and worked to find an empty slot next week for another booking. Why people wanted to be outside to take pictures during the hot summer months was beyond me, but it wasn't my job to give them my opinions on weather.

Later than normal, Nacha walked up with Hank in tow. They stood outside the studio, forgetting that the entire front was one giant window. Didn't they do enough kissing at home?

Hank pushed open the door and waved at me. "You coming tomorrow night?"

"I'll be there. I wouldn't miss the pool party." Hank and his friend Zach threw some of the best parties I'd ever attended. Missing was not an option.

Nacha kissed her husband one more time before patting his chest. "Go get your doughnuts. I'll see you later."

"Love you." He whistled as he walked down the sidewalk.

"Morning. Sorry I'm late. Any issues?" She adjusted the camera bag on her shoulder.

"It's all good. I booked a couple more sessions. And I'm getting ready to file some stuff Haley gave me yesterday."

"Great. I need to tackle a few things; then I'll show you

the best ones from last night. I haven't edited everything, but there are lots of great options."

"Yay. Exactly what I wanted to hear. I can't wait to see them." I winced when I thought of what my daddy would say if he saw my picture on the cover of a leopard shifter romance.

Luckily, that wasn't his favorite genre.

* * *

NACHA WAVED as she walked out the door at the end of the workday. This was the worst part for me. Being alone. I wasn't good at it, so I grabbed my purse and headed next door. The shop had been closed since three, but I knew Tessa was still inside.

She unlocked the door and swung it open. "Hiya. I don't have anything left. Customers wiped me out today."

"I don't need a doughnut. Just company. What are you doing tonight?"

"Nothing special. Want to come over?" She wiped down counters.

"Yes. If you don't mind. I get tired of being alone in that tiny little apartment."

She took off her apron. "We can ask Delaney to join us."

"Sounds good to me." I pulled my phone out of my purse. "Hang on. Let me get a shot of your apron hanging like that." I pressed the button, then showed Tessa the picture. "That will be perfect in your feed." I uploaded the photo, then added a caption. *Hanging up the apron at the end of the day. We'll be open early with more doughnuts in the morning.*

"I don't know how you know what to post. The response has been amazing. I get messages all the time, and I've even had a few people drive out from San Antonio because they follow my page."

"Yay! People like feeling connected. And seeing pictures fuels that connection."

She grinned. "You're a natural at this. But you rarely post on your own page."

"I don't think Mom and Daddy check this stuff, but just in case, I keep it very tame. And it's not like my life is wild."

"Just a little crazy."

"A little. A picture in my leopard suit would have been awesome." I shrugged. "But I'd rather not have my parents quit talking to me completely."

"I'm sure they'd never do that."

I wasn't as sure.

After Tessa finished cleaning up, we knocked on Delaney's door. The lights were already turned off, but a glow appeared in the back as the office door opened, and Delaney ran to the front. "Hey, what's up?"

"Want to hang out at Tessa's?"

"Sure. Give me about ten more minutes, and then I'll head that way."

Tessa smiled. "Great. You know where it is."

We all went in separate directions, and I called back over my shoulder, "I'll pick up ice cream."

I drove to the little mom-and-pop market two streets over. Walking probably would've been a better choice, but I didn't think of it until I was halfway there. Stadtburg wasn't a big place, but it was growing. They'd even put in a new neighborhood down the road. Only half of the lots had houses on them so far. Probably not for long. New houses were being built all the time.

Haley sometimes talked about the old days when they knew everyone else in town. Now that it was more of a suburb, it wasn't that way.

I bought a few pints of ice cream in a variety of fun flavors because I definitely wasn't in a vanilla sort of mood.

ONE CHOICE I'D NEVER MAKE

Then I detoured through the new neighborhood on my way to Tessa's apartment. If I could figure out how to make more money, maybe I'd get one of these houses.

Anything would be better than that tiny room, incorrectly labeled as an apartment. I mean, I was grateful for the place to live, but the space made me claustrophobic. And it didn't even have a kitchen, only a mini fridge and a sink. I was grateful for a sink that wasn't in the bathroom.

At a stop sign, as I rolled to a stop, a guy—who didn't happen to be wearing a shirt—jogged past my car. He was wiping his face, so I stayed there until I could get a peek at what I guessed was a handsome face.

Staring, I didn't notice the car behind me. And just as the jogger lowered the shirt he'd used to wipe his face, the impatient person behind me started honking.

The bare-chested jogger looked a lot like my hero. Ugh. I was losing my mind.

I pulled away from the stop sign before the car behind me could lay on the horn again, but I glanced in the rearview mirror a time or two.

It couldn't be the same guy. We were miles from downtown San Antonio.

Just in case, I drove around the block. Scanning the sidewalk, I searched for my hero look-alike. Either he'd vanished, or he'd gone inside one of the houses.

Knocking on every door was a possibility, but then my ice cream would melt.

I continued to Tessa's apartment, thinking that maybe tomorrow I'd take a walk in this neighborhood. On this block. Back and forth.

Or maybe a trip to the local fire station wasn't a bad idea. I could take them doughnuts.

CHAPTER 3

*A*fter I'd stayed up way too late and consumed copious amounts of ice cream, Saturday morning disappeared before I made it out of bed. If I wanted to take a walk in that neighborhood—and hunt for my superhero—I'd have to do it in the heat.

If I found him, I'd be a sweaty mess. That would make finding him counterproductive. I could just imagine how that conversation would go.

"Hi, remember me? The leopard who lost her tail. Want to hug me again? I'm only a little bit sweaty."

And now, I was talking to myself... out loud. I'd completely lost it.

I grabbed a breakfast bar, changed into my cutest workout clothes, and drove down the road. On the same street where my mystery man disappeared, I parked along the curb.

With my hair pulled up into a cute ponytail, I popped in my earbuds and took off down the sidewalk. Looking cute was my main goal.

As I walked, people waved and called out pleasantries.

Small-town life was so different from where I'd grown up. In my neighborhood back home, the only people who smiled and responded to my greetings were the cleaning ladies and delivery people.

That was one big reason I didn't want to move back home. I just had to keep my parents happy enough that they wouldn't cut me off completely. If I played my cards right, their monthly donations to funding my life would resume. I could only hope.

Looking at every house as I passed it, I walked to the end of the block, then back again. I stopped at my car for a sip of water. Getting too hot would make me sweat.

"Ahem. You aren't supposed to be parked here."

I recognized the voice. It wasn't my handsome hero. It was the handsome deputy who wasn't at all interested. I didn't mind. He wasn't my type... other than the good-looking part.

"Hey, Eli. Why can't I park here?"

He pointed at the No Parking sign right next to my car. Why hadn't I noticed that?

"There isn't parking allowed on this side of the street."

"Why not? That's silly."

He flipped open his little ticket thing. "I don't make the rules. I just enforce them."

I couldn't afford a ticket, especially not after all the ice cream I bought last night. "I'll move my car then. Can I park on the other side of the street?"

He looked up from his little book of tickets and nodded. "Other side doesn't have any signs forbidding it."

"I'm sorry about that. I didn't even see the sign." I needed to find Eli a nice girl because he might be less tightly wound if he had a sweetheart. A little casual conversation would hopefully ease the tension. "Are you going to Hank and Nacha's later?"

"Yep. Should be fun." He closed his little book. "I guess I'll see you there." He tipped his cowboy hat and walked back to his car.

"Eli, wait!"

Since he was a deputy, there was a good chance he knew almost everyone in this town, so why not pick his brain?

"Do you perhaps know of a fireman who lives on this block?"

He laughed. "I'm a deputy, not a dating service. Have a good day, and don't forget to read signs."

He didn't deserve a sweetheart after that snark.

I parked my car on the opposite side of the street, then waited until Eli was out of sight before running across the street. I didn't want him giving me a ticket for jaywalking.

After two more laps up and down the sidewalk, I gave up. If the man I saw jogging lived anywhere near here, he was in hiding. I needed to find food, decide what swimsuit to wear to the party, then get ready. And I only had three hours.

I needed to hurry.

* * *

THE NEXT TIME Nacha hosted a pool party, I'd have to see if I could invite my new friends, Tessa and Delaney, because right now Eli and I were the only two singles. And I was not interested in Eli.

He sat down in the chair next to me. "You ever find your fireman?"

"I don't want to talk about it." I still hadn't mentioned my embarrassing moment to Haley and Nacha, and I definitely didn't want to do it with an audience. "Is there any tea inside?"

"Unsweetened."

"Ick." I dipped a potato chip in french onion dip. "Since

you're single, I could introduce you to someone. You know, if you want."

"I don't want. But thanks." Eli stood and walked toward the pool.

My plan worked as intended, but I wasn't done. "Why not? I have some nice friends. Do you know Tessa?"

"At the bakery?" A snarky smile spread across his face.

Of course he knew Tessa. He was a deputy, and she sold doughnuts.

"Yes. That Tessa."

"I know her." He tugged off his shirt. "She's my cousin." With barely a splash, he dove under the water.

I was either losing my touch, or today was not my day.

Hank poked his head out the door. "Can I get you anything to drink?"

"Sweet tea."

He shook his head. "Don't have any. Sorry."

"Then I'm good." I tossed my plate into the trash, then slipped off my coverup. Sitting on the edge of the pool, I kicked water at anyone who came near me.

Eli, Zach, and Adam tossed a ball back and forth across the pool. Haley and her friend Eve chatted in lounge chairs. I didn't want to know what Nacha and Hank were doing inside.

I splashed water at Eli as he dove to catch the ball. He wasn't my type, but he was nice to look at. Today, that didn't make me feel better. All the couples looked so happy.

Why had I walked away from the fireman?

Maybe he wasn't a fireman. He could've been a banker who was wearing a borrowed shirt. Nah. He had fireman muscles.

Did bankers even have muscles?

Dragging my toes through the water, I decided that on Monday I'd tell Nacha and Haley about my costumed adventure and ask for their help in locating my missing tail. I hoped that my hero still had it.

"You ordered sweet tea?"

I shaded my eyes as I turned to see who was holding out the red plastic cup. Were my eyes playing tricks on me?

Overjoyed, I launched myself at him. The cups went flying, but I could worry about those later. "My hero!"

His strong arms wrapped around me. "I have something that belongs to you."

"We can talk about that later. I haven't mentioned any of that story to my friends."

His stubble brushed my cheek. "Only one person knows the story. Today is serendipitous."

"I can't believe you're actually here." I didn't want to let go. And there was no way I was risking letting him get away without knowing how to find me. "My name is Cami Phillips, and I work at the photography studio in the strip mall across from the good barbecue place. You know, in case we get separated."

"Good to know." He kept an arm around me and turned as Hank and Nacha walked outside.

Nacha clung to Hank as they made their way into the pool.

"She has issues with water. That's why she hangs on him." I hugged the guy again. "But between you and me, I don't think that's the only reason."

The host couple stepped into the water, and after a few cheers, the party resumed.

My hero guy unbuttoned his shirt. "Go ahead and get in. I'll join you as soon as I clean up the cups."

Staring was probably rude, but I did it anyway. "I think I'll just watch you work."

Haley splashed water at me. "Are you just going to stand there staring at the poor man?"

I flashed her a wide smile and pointed at the guy. "He's a total hottie."

Haley shook her head. "I think as a fireman, he probably hears that a lot."

"You *are* a fireman!" I knew those were fireman muscles.

"In the flesh."

Unable to resist, I patted his chest. "Most definitely."

He threw the cups in the trash, and I splashed water on the area where the tea landed. "It was my fault they fell, and I don't want the patio to get sticky."

"Good idea."

My day had completely turned around. "If I accidentally swallow water in the pool, will you rescue me?"

He smiled like he'd just won a prize. "Absolutely."

"How long would I need to hold my breath before you gave me mouth-to-mouth?" I tugged him toward the pool, then remembered that I didn't even know the man's name. I should at least know his name before I kissed him. And I didn't want the sun to go down before I'd gotten that pleasure. "I'm kidding. Sort of. You know what! I don't even know your name."

"Ethan Harper. Most people call me Harper."

"Harper the hero." I loved the sound of that.

He dove into the pool, and I fanned myself a second just to get a laugh out of Haley and Nacha. What were the chances that the guy I'd bumped into was a friend of theirs?

I loved living in a small town.

CHAPTER 4

*H*arper reached for my hand as we walked out of Nacha's house. "I'd like to see you again."

"That's a relief. I didn't want to have to hunt you down and coincidentally bump into you until you asked me out."

He laughed. "What are you doing tomorrow?"

"Going out with you."

"Perfect. I'm going to need your number." He stopped next to my car. "Oh! Do you want your tail now? I live just down the road."

"I'll get it tomorrow." I leaned back against my car and tilted my head in that perfectly inviting angle. "How did you explain having a tail?"

I couldn't help but wonder who the one person was.

He inched closer. "It's a long story."

"Is it?"

"That's what I'm hoping. The beginning was great. And I'm looking forward to the next chapter." He leaned down and kissed my cheek. "I've thought about you a lot since you hugged me on the sidewalk."

"Ditto." I held out my phone. "Give me your number, and I'll text you mine."

He tapped on the screen, then handed back the phone. "I like the way you titled my contact."

"You are my hero. All flirting aside, when I ran into you that day, I was scared. Seeing you made me feel safe." I rarely admitted when things scared me unless I was making a joke out of it. Growing up, our family always looked like we had it together. Being scared didn't fit with that image.

Neither did wearing a cat suit, but that was another topic altogether.

Before getting into the car, I texted him my number. I added a kissing emoji to the end. Would he get my hint?

He tucked his phone in his pocket after glancing at the screen. "I'll call you."

"I'll be waiting." Desperation wasn't a good look, so I dropped into my driver's seat. I wasn't getting a kiss tonight.

I drove back to my tiny apartment, but not following him took willpower. He'd said he lived just down the road, but I'd learned that just down the road could mean a two-minute walk or a half-hour drive.

AFTER LETTING myself in the backdoor of the office, I closed myself in my tiny apartment. My phone dinged, and I lunged to grab it from my purse.

I had fun tonight. Harper hadn't waited long to send a message which meant he was either texting and driving— and I'd scold him for that—or he lived close to Nacha's house.

Maybe I had seen him jogging down that street.

I did too. And I can't wait to see you again. That wasn't a lie. I'd never been more excited about meeting a guy.

He responded right away. *The barbecue place on Main is open late.*

Let me change out of my swimsuit, and I'll meet you there. I could walk since the place was right across the street.

* * *

I STEPPED into the restaurant and scanned the dining area. After intentionally waiting an extra five minutes, I was surprised Harper wasn't already here.

A hand brushed my back, sending tingles down my spine. "I didn't think we'd have any trouble getting a table, so I waited by the door."

I spun to face Harper. "You look as good as you did in a swimsuit."

"You know what I like about you?"

"I can't wait to hear." I looped my arm around his as we walked to the counter to order.

"Everything."

"You sure know how to make a girl smile."

"How hungry are you?"

"I ate so much at the party. I think I'm going straight for dessert."

He grabbed a tray. "I always have room for barbecue. And Haley says this is the best of the best."

"And she knows her barbecue."

With brisket on his tray, he walked to the register. "Grab whatever you want."

I added a banana pudding to his tray, and then he picked up another.

Once we were seated across from each other at a long, empty table, he smiled. "At the party, we spent lots of time together, but we didn't get much time to talk. Where did you grow up?"

"Houston. But I like living here much better. Houston's great and all, but Stadtburg is really growing on me. And I have friends here. You?"

"Grew up near Dallas. Moved to San Antonio for a job, then to Stadtburg a few months ago when I transferred to this department."

"Do all of you guys work here now?"

"Not Adam, but we're working on him."

Most guys didn't want to hear about my life as an engineer. And living in the back of a photography business and working as a secretary wasn't something I'd put on my dating profile. Maybe he wouldn't ask me about work.

"What do you do?"

There was the question I'd hoped to avoid. But if I couldn't be honest with Harper, we didn't have a chance anyway.

"I used to work as an engineer, but I quit my job because I hated it. Now I answer phones for Haley and Nacha, and I live in the teeny, tiny apartment in the back of the office." I jabbed my spoon into my pudding. "Oh, and I help a couple of my friends with their social media. Impressive, huh?"

"Are you telling me that you've been right next to the doughnut shop this whole time, and I haven't seen you?"

"Which is crazy because I'm in there talking to Tessa almost every morning before work."

"Do you like working for Nacha and Haley?"

"Mostly. There's not really enough for a full-time job, so sometimes I feel like I'm twiddling my thumbs. Other times, I'm buried in phone calls."

"If you could do anything, what would you do?"

I was pretty sure "Kiss you" wasn't the right answer, but it was the first thing that popped into my head. "Not sure. There are so many things I haven't tried. Life is like one of those books where there are different endings and you

ONE CHOICE I'D NEVER MAKE

choose which one to read, and I haven't read through every possible outcome."

"You are like sunshine in designer jeans." He shoved the tray to the side and picked up his pudding. "Siblings?"

"Nope. I'm an only. Daddy's little girl, which comes with its own set of problems. What about you?"

"Three sisters."

"You poor man."

He set the empty container down and reached for my hand. "I'm sure there is probably a joke to be made about chasing tail, but since I'm a nice guy, I won't make it."

"But you'll mention it?"

"I'm mostly nice. Funny too." He brushed his thumb along my fingers. "What would you like to do tomorrow? Indoors or outside?"

"In this heat? Indoors. Please. I truly don't look good when I perspire."

"I'm guessing you always look good, but I'll find us an indoor activity." He glanced up as an employee wiped down tables. "They'll probably ask us to leave soon."

"I'd invite you to my place, but I doubt we'd both fit." I laughed, but it wasn't a lie.

"That's okay. I'll see you tomorrow." He stacked the trash on the tray. "And I'd invite you over, but my roommate is probably crashed on the couch, watching Netflix."

"Tomorrow then."

He squeezed my hand. "Let me drive you home."

CHAPTER 5

Tempering my excitement about a second date with Harper was impossible. After telling Tessa and Delaney all about the barbecue date, I spent the next two hours getting ready.

As I was finishing the final touches on my makeup, my daddy called. It was probably wrong to let it roll to voice mail, but I'd call him back later. Much later. After my date.

Two seconds later, a text popped up on my screen. From Daddy.

I know you stay much too busy to talk to your father, but please call me when you have a chance. Soon preferably. I can only hope you are busy trying to find a new job. One more suited to your degree.

Waiting until after my date would only add irritation to the already uncomfortable situation. I picked up my phone, took a deep breath, and called him back. "Hi, Daddy. I saw that I missed your call. What's up?"

"Camille, have you found a new job?"

"Not yet." I opted not to mention that I wasn't actively looking for one.

He cleared his throat, his way of showing disapproval over the phone. "I hope that changes soon. If you need to move back home—"

"I don't. Really. I'm okay here."

"Working as a receptionist is not okay, Camille. How do you think Mom feels when her friends ask about how you're doing and where you're working? She can avoid the topic only so long."

I could feel the walls of my tiny apartment closing in. "Okay."

"Call me when you have an interview scheduled. We can practice over the phone."

"All right." I kept my voice steady so that he couldn't hear the sobs being held back.

"Talk to you later, sweetheart. Enjoy your Sunday." He ended the call, probably in a hurry to get to brunch before his tee time.

I flopped backward onto the bed. I'd been working this job for months, hoping my parents would eventually give up trying to make life decisions for me. But that was never going to happen.

Moving back home hadn't sounded appealing last week, and now those feelings had multiplied. After bumping into Harper, wild raccoons couldn't drag me back to Houston.

I stood in front of the mirror and dabbed at my eye makeup. Crying wasn't allowed right now. I had a date.

Shoving my tangled knot of emotions into the darkest corner of my brain, I smiled at my own reflection. "Worrying about it today won't change anything. I'll think about it tomorrow."

My phone buzzed, and I giggled at the message from Harper. *I've never picked up a date from a strip mall before. Do I knock at the glass doors or the door in the alley at the back?*

ONE CHOICE I'D NEVER MAKE

In the back. After hitting send on my message, I checked my lipstick. Hopefully, he'd give me reasons to reapply it later… more than once.

I opened the door before he knocked. Patience wasn't my strong suit. "Hi."

His green eyes twinkled. "Howdy. You look fabulous."

Where had he been all my life?

"Before I get all caught up in your compliments, I need to lock up." I could feel him right behind me as I turned the key.

He made it easy not to think about my daddy's call.

I leaned back against his chest. "What's the plan for the day?"

"I hope you aren't allergic to bowling. It's an indoor activity."

"Sounds perfect. But I'm warning you now that I'm not very good at it."

He slid his arms around my waist. "It's just something to do while I'm spending time with you. Stadtburg has a surprising lack of things to do indoors, so we're headed into San Antonio."

"More time to talk."

He clasped my hand and led me to his truck. "Your tail is in my truck. Remind me to give it to you when we get back. I'd hate for you to never be able to wear that outfit again."

I buckled into the seat. "You didn't even ask why I was wearing it."

He winked. "But I can't wait to hear the story."

While he drove, I told him about my part-time modeling. "I've done a few things for local ads, you know, in print or on websites. I also model for book covers. And that was why I was in the leopard suit."

He rubbed the back of his neck. "Book covers, huh?"

"Yeah. It was a little weird at first to think of my face on a book cover somewhere, but I'm dressed in all the pictures. It's not like I'm baring my chest for all the world to see."

His ears turned a vivid red. "I'll have to look up some books you've modeled for."

"Does that embarrass you? Or are your ears red because I was talking about baring my chest?"

"No. Not at all. That's cool." He flashed a disarming smile. "Being on book covers, I mean. What's your favorite color?"

"Today it's red." I brushed my fingers down his arm. "You're really cute."

"I'm glad you think so."

At the bowling alley, I fumbled through the first game, knocking over fewer pins than I could count on my fingers and toes. But laughter abounded. On my final turn, I picked up the bowling ball, then glanced back over my shoulder. "Do you give lessons?"

He grinned and strolled up to me. "I'll do my best."

His breath tickled my ear as he gave me instructions on when to swing the ball back and when to release it. Rather than actually listening, I was enjoying the feel of his hand on my waist and his fireman muscles right up against me.

"Think you can do that?"

"Uh-huh." I lifted the ball into the classic bowling stance, then swung it and let it fly down the… gutter. "Your handsomeness is distracting."

He laughed. "Should we play a second game? Or am I too distracting?"

"If you promise to give me a lesson before every turn, I'll play this all day."

"Deal."

He punched the buttons to start a new game. As he took his turn, my phone buzzed, and I made the awful mistake of reading the message.

Your mom invited the Morgans to join us for brunch. Mr.

Morgan has an open position. He said to call and schedule an interview. Mostly as a formality. He's excited about having you join his company. Daddy knew how to ruin a perfect date.

I blinked my frustration back into its closet, then smiled as Harper threw his arms in the air. Another strike. He was good at this game.

"Maybe you should try a lighter ball. That might help you." He studied my face. "Is everything okay?"

"Oh, yeah. Let me see what I can find." Looking for another ball was a great excuse to get a minute alone and corral my emotions.

I picked up balls one by one until I found a bright green ball that felt light enough. My fingers kind of stuck in the holes a bit. But I didn't have to hold the ball long. I walked up to the lane, and Harper stepped up behind me and repeated his mini lesson. This time, I listened.

"Just be careful not to let go too soon." He tightened his arms around my waist. "And if this isn't fun anymore, just say the word."

"By *this*, do you mean you? If so, I'm having oodles of fun." I closed my eyes for a second remembering his instructions. "I can do this."

I walked up to the lane swung the ball back, reminding myself not to let go too soon, then swung the ball. My brain never got to the part about letting go. It didn't help that my fingers were wedged into the holes. And the ball didn't feel that light anymore.

The ball flew down the lane with me attached. My face slammed against the floor, and the screech of my skin skidding along the polished lane drew unwanted attention. When I stopped sliding I wrenched the ball free and shoved it down the lane.

Pins scattered as the ball crashed into them. With my eyes closed, I rubbed my temples.

As I pushed up, hands grabbed my hips.

"Don't go that direction. You don't want to get caught in that machine."

Standing in the bowling lane, I threw my arms around Harper and buried my face in the curve of his neck. "You saved me again."

"I think we've bowled enough for one day… maybe enough for the year. Let's go find you an ice pack and get something to eat."

"Sounds good."

He helped me up, waving off the crowds asking if I was okay. "She's fine. Just took a tumble."

I picked up my purse and headed toward the door.

"Wait up, Cami. I need to pay before we go."

With my cheek throbbing, I nodded but didn't stop walking. Harper was one of the reasons I didn't want to move back home, but I'd royally messed up this relationship. It was one thing to be fun-loving. It was something else entirely to go sliding down a bowling lane.

It could've been worse. I could've been in a dress instead of shorts.

While my brain was busy thinking about how badly I'd messed up, my foot caught on something, and I lunged forward, sending my purse flying and my face heading back toward the ground.

Strong arms caught me. Harper pulled me close a second before saying anything. "Wait here. Let me pick up what fell."

Without a hint of embarrassment, that man picked up the contents of my purse that had scattered all over the floor… including my feminine products.

He handed me the purse. "Where would you like to eat?"

Overwhelmed with pain, embarrassment, and that stupid text, I knew being around me wouldn't be any fun, but I couldn't even look Harper in the eye. "I think I just want to go home."

"All right." He stayed next to me as I walked to the truck, but he didn't reach for my hand or put his arm around me.

I'd messed up everything.

CHAPTER 6

Crying, I flopped onto the bed.

Harper had promised to call, but he was probably just being nice. I wouldn't blame him if he didn't.

I'd only been home a few minutes when someone knocked at the back door. Tessa and Delaney always texted before coming over. The only person who knocked on that door was Eli when he was making his rounds.

He didn't like the idea of a single woman living in a strip mall. Not that it was any of his business.

I ignored the first knock but knew better than to ignore the second. I didn't need him calling Haley and Nacha.

Wiping my eyes, I yanked open the door. "Eli, you don't have to—"

Harper held out a milkshake. "Should I be worried that you assumed my roommate was knocking at the door? And I took a guess that you'd want chocolate with extra whipped cream and a cherry."

My tears started again, but now they fell for an entirely different reason. "You brought me a milkshake."

"My mom swore that milkshakes could cure anything. At

least when I was a kid. And I brought you this." He handed me an ice pack.

"Where did you find a store that sells them already frozen?" It sounded dumber when I said it out loud.

He chuckled. "I grabbed it from my freezer. Now, back to the Eli part."

My brain jumped from confusion to anger. "That stinker is your roommate?"

"He is. I met him through—"

"Zach. Yeah, I know how all that small-town stuff works. It's weird. And Eli knocks whenever he does his rounds. You aren't seriously worried that there's anything going on with us, are you?"

Harper laughed. "Nope. Eli talks to you. And when Eli is attracted to someone, he can't string a full sentence together. We give him a hard time about that. So, no. I'm not worried."

"Do you want to come in?" I liked my fireman a little more every time I saw him.

He stepped closer and trailed a thumb across what was probably a bruise. "I'd love to. Let me grab my shake from the truck."

I sat cross-legged on the bed, and Harper dropped into the one comfy chair in the small space.

"I'm not a mind reader, but something changed right before you fell. Is everything okay?"

"Sort of." I tried to decide how much of my dirty laundry to air this early in the relationship. My actual dirty laundry had been kicked under the bed when he ran to grab his shake.

"I hope you intend to say more than that."

"My parents aren't happy with my job or where I live or any of my recent choices for that matter. And my daddy texted that his buddy has a job for me."

Harper slouched back into the chair. "You're moving to Houston?"

"Heavens no. I just need to figure out how to smooth things over without becoming everything I hate. Maybe there's a self-help book for that. *How to Tell Your Parents NO and Not Get Cut Off.*" So much for carefully choosing my words.

"It would be a hit."

"Sorry I'm being a downer."

"You aren't, Cami. I'm glad you told me what was bothering you. I thought maybe I smelled bad."

"Not at all."

I held the ice pack to the side of my face. "Did you always want to be a fireman?"

"Pretty much. When I was five, a house down the street caught fire. I stood outside for hours watching the fireman battle the blaze. Ever since that day, I knew what I wanted to be when I grew up."

"I think you were born to be a firefighter and to rescue people." I slurped the last of the chocolate from the bottom of my cup. "I wasn't sure you'd call me."

He set his cup on my dresser and walked toward the bed. "You got away from me once. I didn't want that to happen again."

Then Harper brushed his lips on mine with all the gentleness of a bomb-squad guy defusing a bomb. The result inside my brain was more like the bomb exploding.

"I've been hoping you would do that."

"I've been wanting to. You should keep ice on that bruise, and I'm not helping you do that when I'm kissing you." He moved back to his chair. "Anything I can do to help with the job thing?"

"Not really. I've been thinking about finding something else because this place is so small, but I can't afford much with what I'm paid." I waggled my finger at him. "That is not a dig at Haley and Nacha. I'll figure it out. I just won't reply to the text for a few days, then when Daddy calls, I'll realize he didn't give me the number to call, then I just won't call. That's pretty much my plan."

"What could go wrong with that?" Harper scrunched up his nose as if he were imagining the long list of things that could go wrong with my plan.

"Exactly. Is the invitation to get food still a possibility?"

"Always." He laced his fingers with mine when I stepped next to him.

Was it too soon to be in love? Because on a scale of one to ten, my hero was a five hundred and three.

* * *

AFTER DINNER as I tried to unlock the door, Harper tapped my head with the leopard tail. "You can't forget this. I know I won't."

I spun around before opening the door. "Who knew about what happened?"

He rested his hands on the doorframe and leaned closer to me. "I decided not to mention it when I met everyone at dinner that night. It sounded too crazy to be true. A woman throwing her arms around me and calling me a hero? Who would've believed it? I did tell Eli about it. How else was I supposed to explain why I was bringing home a tail?"

"I saw you jogging the day before the party. I'm almost sure it was you."

"And you didn't chase me?"

"Apparently, it's bad form to park at a stop sign and run down the street."

Chuckling, he closed the distance between us and kissed me. This kiss would definitely mess up my lipstick.

"Goodnight, Cami."

"Thank you for coming back."

He smiled. "Anytime you need a milkshake, you know who to call."

I leaned on the door as he walked to his truck. The throbbing in my cheek had subsided, but now my heart felt like it might explode.

My phone started buzzing when I walked inside. Expecting the worst, I checked my messages. It wasn't Daddy. Tessa and Delaney wanted the full scoop.

I sent off a message to both of them. *Video chat or should we meet somewhere?*

Tessa replied first. *I'm putting cookies in the oven now. Come on over.*

I grabbed my purse and ran out the door but stopped and sent another text. *I have a bruise. Don't be alarmed. Will explain.*

The last thing I needed was them thinking Harper had hit me. He was the one who'd saved me from being reset like a bowling pin. It wasn't as if I was that close to getting caught in the machine, but he still steered me away from it.

And after that last kiss, I was more determined than ever to ward off the wild raccoons that wanted to drag me back home.

CHAPTER 7

*L*ast night, I'd told my friends all about how great Harper was... and about the phone call and text that almost ruined my whole date.

Tessa and Delaney both agreed that Harper was a keeper. Sadly, they had no advice to offer about the parental situation.

And now, I would get to update Haley and Nacha.

At my desk a few minutes early, I was there to greet them both when they walked in.

Haley's eyes widened, and Nacha gasped.

The bruise.

"First of all, this"—I motioned to my face—"wasn't Harper's fault."

Haley shook her head. "I didn't think it was. But now I'm really curious how Harper came up in this conversation."

That was when my brain caught up. "Didn't I mention we went out yesterday?"

"I haven't seen you since you left my house. I mean, I'm not at all surprised you went out, but you still haven't said how you ended up with that nasty bruise." Nacha rubbed her stomach, then pulled a sleeve of saltines out of her purse.

"Bowling. It's best to let go of the ball when you throw it down the lane. Staying attached is not recommended."

"Ouch." Haley set her purse in a chair. "How did the date go otherwise?"

"Harper is pretty much awesomeness with extra muscles."

Nacha wiped cracker crumbs off her mouth. "And now you can tell us how you first met him. From your reaction to him, it must've been quite a story."

"When I was walking back to my car in the leopard suit after that photo shoot, there was someone following me."

"I knew we should have walked with you." Haley shook her head.

"Well, I saw Harper near the parking lot and hugged him and whispered that I was being followed. He acted like we were old friends and that he was happy to see me."

"I bet he was *very* happy to see you." Haley laughed.

"Turns out the guy following me was only trying to return my tail. It had fallen out of my purse."

Nacha spit cracker crumbs all over the floor, then covered her mouth. "Sorry."

"Yeah. Then I bolted."

"You left Harper standing there?" Haley laughed.

"I did, but I left my tail. Anyway, by the next morning, I greatly regretted leaving, but I had no idea where to find my green-eyed hero. Then fate took over."

Haley rolled her eyes. "I'm glad you found him."

"Me too."

"I've got to get some work done." Nacha headed into her office.

"Ditto." Haley picked up her purse. "We can only hope it's quiet today."

I stared out the window as a firetruck pulled into the lot. Guys piled out, probably headed for the doughnut shop.

Harper stopped outside the studio and winked.

I blew him a kiss, then waved.

It was weird to be so happy and on the brink of being completely and totally broke.

Trying to focus on work, I answered the phone and scheduled another session in the heat of summer.

As soon as I hung up, Haley slapped money onto the desk. "Would you mind running next door and getting me coffee? Pretty please."

With the money in my fist, I ran toward the door. "Be back in a bit."

Laughter echoed behind me as I darted outside.

When I walked into the doughnut shop, I scanned the group of firemen. No Harper. Then I looked at all the tables. Where was he?

An arm circled my waist. "I texted your boss and told her that she needed to send you for coffee."

"So you orchestrated this meeting." I spun to face him.

"I wanted to see you." He nodded toward the counter. "What would you like?"

"A chocolate-covered one with sprinkles." I was gaining an even deeper appreciation for small towns.

When the other guys finished ordering, Harper stepped up to the counter and told Tessa what we wanted.

Standing just behind him, I waved at Tessa. At this point, it was unlikely she hadn't figured out who he was. In fact, she probably saw him in here all the time. It was a wonder I hadn't met Harper weeks ago.

She grinned.

When Harper had his order, he handed me a coffee and my doughnut. "For Haley. Give her my thanks. Want to sit for a minute?"

"I should get back over there, but it was nice bumping into you." I nudged his shoulder with mine.

He pushed open the door. "I'll walk with you."

I stopped outside the studio, feeling guilty that I'd ever laughed at Nacha and Haley for kissing their husbands on the sidewalk. Now, I understood and was hoping Harper would give the ladies a reason to poke fun at me.

My fireman didn't disappoint.

When he leaned down, holding a coffee cup in one hand and a doughnut in the other, I slipped my arms around his neck, trying not to spill hot coffee down his back. His lips danced against mine a minute before he pulled away. "Unless tonight is crazy, I'll call you later."

"Can't wait." I opened the door. "I hope I didn't get chocolate in your hair."

"I'm sure the guys will tell me if you did." He stole one more peck before I walked back inside.

I set the cup on Haley's desk. "Thanks."

She laughed. "Was I supposed to say no? Someone seems smitten, and I don't mean you."

"I hope so. I should probably be more sensible about this, but whenever he's near me, I feel like I'm about to melt."

"I know the feeling. With Zach it was the same way." She reached for her camera bag and coffee. "I'm headed out to do a shoot. If I need to cover Nacha's afternoon shoot, text me. I don't think she's feeling great."

"Wait! Let me snap a picture. That's a great shot to let people know you are off on a shoot. Have you thought about doing short videos about taking better photos?"

"Still thinking about it. Call or text if you need me."

"I will." I dropped into my chair and broke my doughnut in half. Taking alternating bites out of each half, I kept the pieces approximately even in size until one half disappeared completely. Then I got back to work.

After an hour, I'd finished all my tasks, and the phone was quiet. While Nacha was squirreled away in her office, I scanned the Want Ads. Maybe I'd find something I could do part-time.

CHAPTER 8

Sitting on my bed, I poured dressing on my salad. I deserved a medal. I'd been off work for almost an hour, and I hadn't gone to the fire station.

Eating takeout wasn't saving me any money, but without a kitchen, I didn't have a lot of choices. My easy go-to meal was a salad. I stocked my minifridge with healthy stuff. Yay me!

I hadn't given much thought to how to respond to my daddy. He was probably getting antsy. How could I stand up for myself without ruining everything? They were my parents. As much as I joked about the money, the real issue wasn't getting cut off financially.

I wanted them to be proud of their only daughter, but the person they wanted me to be wasn't me. And I had no idea how to tell them that without seeing disappointment on their faces.

My phone buzzed, and I scattered salad everywhere when I lunged to grab it.

"Hello?" My excitement about talking to Harper washed away when I heard my mom's voice.

"Hi, sweetheart. Your father and I are in San Antonio. Where should we meet you?"

"Um, you're where?"

"We're not quite to downtown right now. Send me an address for a restaurant. Hurry."

"Okay." My brain blanked out, and my stomach churned. "Let me hang up and get the address."

I didn't want them anywhere near where I lived. They didn't know that part of my situation.

After texting Mom the address of a restaurant in San Antonio, I tossed my salad into the trash and pulled on my shoes.

Maybe I'd think of a great idea while I was driving into town. Not likely.

They beat me to the restaurant. I'm not sure why that mattered, but now it felt like their turf.

When I walked inside, I didn't miss the determination on Daddy's face. He was the wild raccoon. But I was not going home.

Faking a smile—a skill I'd mastered growing up—I hugged each of them. "This is a surprise."

Mom slapped a hand to her chest. "Your face. Who hit you?"

Anger flashed in Daddy's eyes.

I put my hands up in front of me, hoping that gesture would calm them down. Did that ever work? "No one hit me. I fell when I went bowling."

His eyes narrowed. "Are you dating someone new?"

This was absolutely not the time to answer that question. "Daddy, I fell. Honest."

Mom trailed a finger over the bruise. "I might have a better concealer in my purse."

"It's fine, Mom." I pulled my face away from her hand.

Daddy alerted the hostess that we were ready to be

seated, then turned his focus back to me. "You never answered my text."

"About that—"

He held up a finger. "We're not going to discuss it standing here."

Then why bring it up when we were standing here? I hated his control tactics.

Mom smiled. "How was work today?"

"Good." And I hated the play-nice game.

The hostess shot me a look of pity. "Right this way."

I followed my parents to the table and took a seat across from Daddy.

The waiter hurried up to the table before we'd opened the menus. "What can I get y'all to drink?"

"I'll have a Topo Chico with lime."

Mom furrowed her brow. "Water with lemon."

Daddy didn't even look at the poor guy. "Same and a black coffee."

I flashed the man an extra smile. He'd drawn the short straw tonight. My parents would not be happy customers.

Once the drinks arrived and we ordered food, Daddy looked at me. "Do you need me to hire movers for you?"

"I'm not moving." My words came out in barely a whisper.

Mom shook her head. "Is there a boy that's keeping you here? I just don't understand. Chase would love to have you back in Houston."

Chase was my ex for a reason. And he was on the list of reasons I wasn't still in Houston. And tonight was not the time to talk about Harper.

Daddy would make my feelings sound like a playground crush or find Harper and harass him, thinking he'd given me the bruise.

My phone buzzed, and I didn't even pull it out of my purse.

"I like living in Stadtburg. I have friends here. I'm happy here."

What parents didn't want their child to be happy? Mine, apparently.

Daddy had been quiet. Too quiet. And when he glanced up, the look on his face scared me. "You are happy to take money from us, but you don't want to take our advice. That's not how it's going to be."

The waiter walked up, carrying a tray loaded with plates. He quietly set our food on the table. "If you need anything else, my name is Ethan."

It was as if the universe was poking me.

"Thank you." Mom acted like her family wasn't imploding.

I picked up my fork.

Daddy pointed at me. "That SUV you drive and the phone that keeps buzzing in your purse—I paid for those. I'm giving you two weeks. That's enough time to give notice at work."

"Two weeks or what?"

"You want to stay here? Find an engineering job in town. Otherwise, there is one waiting for you in Houston. I'll be back in two weeks to hear what you decide."

"So you're saying—"

"I'm taking the car, the phone, and the designer clothes hanging in your closet. All the stuff that I paid for."

So much for eating.

I stared at my plate.

My mom sighed. "Now that we are done with that conversation, have you talked to Chase lately? He got a promotion recently."

"I haven't talked to him since I handed him the ring back." Usually that ended small talk about Chase.

Twenty-five, I had a string of stupid decisions under my belt. Thankfully, I figured out Chase's philandering ways before I'd marched down the aisle. Then I'd dated my boss and gotten dumped.

It was amazing I could order dinner for myself without messing up.

"Nora, Camille isn't going to marry Chase. He's not good for her." Daddy smiled at me. "I do want the best for you." The man was complicated.

Through the rest of dinner, Mom filled me in on the comings and goings of all my former schoolmates. Most of them were married or engaged. And the single ones all had fabulous jobs.

Daddy barely said a word.

Even though my stomach was in knots, I ate because Daddy was paying, and my budget was tight.

Hopefully, the food wouldn't come back up later.

* * *

THE TEARS POURING out of my eyes made it hard to drive home. And the flashing lights in my rearview mirror compounded my problems.

After coming to a complete stop on the side of the road, I rolled my window down.

Eli cocked his head as he walked up. "What's wrong?"

If I told Eli what was wrong, he'd tell Harper, and I wasn't ready to talk to him about it. I didn't even want to think about it.

"I'm fine. Was I speeding?"

"No. You're driving a little slow, but the swerving is why I pulled you over."

"Sorry. I was getting a tissue out of my purse."

He closed his little ticket book. "Think you can make it home in one piece?"

I nodded without looking at him.

"You can go." He strolled back to his car.

How long before he called Harper? Did guys pass information like that? Rather than staying on the side of the road, watching to see if Eli called anyone, I drove home.

My phone buzzed as I walked inside. I had my answer.

I took a deep breath and answered in my chipper voice. "Hey, what's up?"

"I'm guessing whatever is wrong can't be fixed by a milkshake." Harper's voice was as comforting as his arms.

"I wish, but nope."

"Want to talk about—" A clanging alarm sounded in the background. "I'll call you later."

Saved by the bell. I didn't want to talk to him about it. This was a decision I had to make on my own.

This was like the final exam in the school of adulthood, and I hadn't studied. I didn't even have a textbook.

CHAPTER 9

My head hurt when I opened my eyes. Who was knocking at the door?

Avoiding the mirror—I didn't need to see my reflection to know I looked awful—I yanked open the back door.

Harper held out a doughnut and a cup of coffee. "Tessa said to call her later."

"I guess everyone knows I'm upset about something."

"Not everyone. Lots of people are still asleep and haven't seen their messages."

"Funny. Come on in but don't look at me."

"Anything I can do?"

"Nope."

"I'm gonna go out on a limb and guess that your plan about how to deal with that text went awry."

"Good guess. But honestly, I don't want to talk about it. How was work?"

"Busy. I've had better shifts."

I set my doughnut and coffee on the dresser, then wrapped him in a hug. "I'm sorry."

He chuckled. "I didn't say it to get sympathy, but now that I know it works…"

"That's what I like about you. You're funny. You probably didn't get much sleep last night."

"Some. Based on the puffiness of your eyes that I perceived without looking at you, crying took up more of your night than sleeping."

"Yep. But I'll figure things out." I wasn't going to be the new girlfriend who begged for help. "If I did, you know, move back to Houston… would you visit me?"

"I would." He nodded but didn't look up. His actions screamed louder than his words.

I hated seeing disappointment on faces when I was the cause. "You don't have to say that. I'd understand if you don't want to date someone who lives on the other side of the state."

He met my gaze. "You aren't just someone."

My crying started again.

Harper held me until I managed to catch my breath.

"Sorry. I promise I'm not usually like this. You can ask Nacha and Haley. I almost never cry. It's just…" I shrugged and shut up before more tears spewed from my eyes.

"I like to think it's because you trust me enough not to hide your feelings."

"Oh my word! What romance novel did you walk out of?"

His ears turned red again. "Sisters, remember? I have notecards in my wallet with all the things ladies like to hear. Wanna see?"

I laughed, and it was as satisfying as warm hot chocolate. "Have a seat. I'm not going to dump all my troubles on you, but I appreciate you coming to check on me and being so sweet." I broke my doughnut in half. "I've known you less than a week, and I'm already crying on your shoulder. Red flag! Run away."

"Should I be jealous of Eli?" He narrowed his eyes, making it hard to tell if there was humor sparkling in those green pools. The question had come out of nowhere. Was he trying to be funny? I couldn't risk letting him think there was anyone else.

"What? No! I mean, I sort of went on a bit about how he was good looking, but he's so not my type. He's like that cousin who teases a little bit but sticks up for you if someone else picks on you. So, no. Absolutely no reason to be jealous."

He laughed. "Just making sure."

Laughter lightened the mood.

"Is there anyone I should be jealous of?" I stared at my pieces of doughnut, trying to remember which one I'd bitten off last.

Harper paled. "No. Haley and I only went out once. A blind date. Did I mention that Zach was there too?"

I slapped a hand over my mouth in time to keep doughnut chunks from flying out. "Poor you. A third wheel on your own blind date."

"Exactly. Now that we've cleared all that out of the way, what are you doing for dinner tonight?"

"I don't have any plans."

"I'll make you dinner. I'm learning some new skills." He covered a yawn. "I'm about to turn into a pumpkin. I should go."

"Dinner sounds awesome. And risky. What time should I be there?"

He leaned down and hovered his lips near mine. "I'll pick you up after work."

I pressed my lips to his.

I'd miss this. Terribly.

* * *

Haley and Nacha showed up to work early.

Instead of waiting for them to awkwardly ask why I'd been sobbing, I said, "I'm having personal problems. I don't really want to talk about it because I have to figure it out on my own."

Nacha lifted her eyebrows. "We're your friends, Cami. If you need help, we're here."

"Thank you."

Haley hugged me. "Run next door for a bit. I'll cover the phones."

"Harper is home sleeping." I figured both of them probably already knew he'd been over here first thing this morning.

The gossip chain in this town was alive and well. Was it really gossip when my friends were worried about me?

"I figured you'd want to chat with Tessa and Delaney. You didn't get over there this morning, and they are worried about you." Haley held up her coffee. "Ask me how I know."

"I'll go over there for a few minutes. And just so you know, I'm not going to talk to them about my problems, so don't feel like you're being left out. Seriously. It has to be my decision." I walked out of the studio and into the bakery.

Delaney and Tessa looked up from where they were chatting at a table.

"I'm okay. I'm in a bit of a fix, but I don't want to talk about it." I crossed my arms.

Tessa shook her head. "We don't want to hear about your problems. We want to hear about Harper. I can't believe he's the guy you left your tail with. He comes in here all the time." She winked.

Friends like these were golden. I'd miss them too.

I sat down at the table and told them all about my hero who knew exactly what to say and when. The only part I left out was about moving away.

While I was leaning toward that decision—because how was I supposed to live without a car and my clothes and a phone—I'd go home, kicking and screaming.

But I didn't want to go at all.

My head hurt from thinking about it.

CHAPTER 10

I tucked the stack of flat boxes out of sight before Harper showed up. I'd run to get them on my lunch break, then snuck them inside after Haley and Nacha went home.

One way or the other, I was packing my clothes.

Harper texted that he was on his way. I had about two minutes to change clothes before he pulled up. I slipped out of my work clothes and pulled on shorts and a cute top.

I wanted to spend as much time with him as possible.

When he knocked, I yanked open the door. "Hi."

He brushed my cheek. "This already looks better."

"It feels better." Before walking to his truck, I locked the door. "What are you making tonight?"

"Lasagna. It's all prepped and waiting to go into the oven." He clasped my hand. "We'll have to wait forty-five minutes until we can eat."

"Whatever will we do?" Without letting go of his hand, I turned to face him. "I'm stunned that you cook."

"As I said, I'm learning. I got this recipe from my little sister. She said it was foolproof. Actually she said it was guy-proof." He winked. "She's joking though. Her husband is a trained chef."

"I love that you get recipes from your sister. Are you close to all of them? Are they all married?"

"My youngest sister married recently. My other sisters are both married and have kids." He parked in his driveway. "And I talk to them a couple of times a month. I facetime with my nephew and nieces when I can. I don't want them to forget me since I live far away."

"Aww. How cute is that?"

He winked and tapped his back pocket. "Notecards."

I looped my arm around his. "Sometimes I can't tell if you're joking."

"I love your smile. Have I told you that?"

"Is that written on one of those notecards?"

He shook his head as he pushed open the front door. "This is my place. Make yourself at home."

There was almost nothing on the walls. All the furniture looked comfortable. My mom would not have approved.

"It suits you. Definitely looks like guys live here. How did you end up rooming with Eli? And I'm mad at him, by the way. The day after I thought I saw you, I came over here and walked up and down the street. Eli almost gave me a ticket for parking on the wrong side of the street, but anyway, I asked him if he knew of any firemen who lived on this block. He laughed it off."

Harper chuckled. "I might have to talk to him about that." He led me into the kitchen and turned on the oven. "What can I get you to drink? I have water, sodas, beer, wine. I assume you are over twenty-one."

I dug through my purse and pulled out my license. "I'm almost twenty-five. How old are you?"

He glanced at it like a bouncer at a club. "Thirty-one."

"So, you're like a real grown-up?"

"I suppose so. I have a job. I own a house and a truck. I guess that qualifies me for the adulting club."

I stepped closer to him. "I'll have a glass of wine."

Now more than ever, I wasn't going to unleash my problems on Harper. The last thing I wanted was for him to think I was after his money. He was the picture of stability. I was chaos in designer clothes.

But only for a couple more weeks. Then I'd just be chaos.

Even if Harper turned out to be a summer crush, I'd learned something from him. Handling life as an adult was attractive, and running home was not going to teach me anything about growing up.

He handed me a glass of wine. "I see those wheels turning. Care to share?"

"I'm not going to fill our evening with the bleh of what's going on in my life. I know you're willing to listen, and I'll tell you more about it in a day or two. Right now, I just want you to know that I'm not leaving Stadtburg. Well, not moving back to Houston."

His green eyes twinkled, but there was concern pinched at the corners. "I'm happy to hear that."

"Tell me more about your family."

He popped the top on a Coke, then motioned toward the living room. "I'll tell you anything you want to know. But first, I need to know if you're safe. After what happened bowling and then finding you in tears, I'm concerned. The talk of moving worried me because it seemed sudden."

"I'm safe. Things are still a mess, but there isn't any reason to be concerned about my safety." I sat down on the couch. "I didn't mean to worry you."

He shrugged. "It's all part of the package. Care and concern go hand in hand."

Being honest would probably relieve some of his worry.

I cradled my wineglass. "Okay, just so you know there is

nothing to worry about, I'll tell you what's going on." I inhaled. "Here goes. I already told you that my parents don't like my choices. My mom thinks I should move back to Houston and marry Chase—I'd rather have bamboo shoved under my fingernails—and my daddy thinks I should be working as an engineer. Bamboo. But because I didn't respond to the text about the fabulous job they've lined up for me, they decided to surprise me. I found out about the surprise when they called and asked where I wanted to meet them for dinner. They'd driven all the way to San Antonio. It wasn't like I could tell them I was busy."

Harper squeezed his can a bit too hard and a dent formed on the side.

"Anyway, Daddy gave me an ultimatum. Is it an ultimatum if I have three options?"

Harper leaned over and kissed the side of my head. "Doesn't matter."

"Basically, I can find an engineering job here in town, move back to Houston and take the job that's waiting for me, or I turn over everything my parents bought me."

The longer Harper stayed quiet, the more I worried that I'd made a horrible mistake by telling him.

"And don't worry. I'm not going to come begging you for money or rides or anything like that. This is my lesson, and I'm determined to learn it." I sipped my wine.

"How long do you have before you give them an answer?"

"Two weeks from yesterday. And I don't want you to think I hate Houston or my parents. It's just that I can't be myself there. But I hate disappointing them."

"I think you're brave, Cami."

"Funny. Especially considering I was afraid of someone who was trying to be a good Samaritan."

"I'll never forget the day you pounced on me."

I swatted his arm. "You make me sound like a cougar."

He chuckled. "You were a leopard."

"Thank you for noticing." I appreciated a man who knew his cats.

Grinning, he nudged my shoulder. "That suit made it easy to notice you."

Instead of turning red and acting embarrassed, I giggled. "I looked good, didn't I? When I give Daddy back all the stuff I bought with his money, that suit will be the exception. I'm keeping it."

"Second best news I've heard all day. Let me check on dinner."

I followed him into the kitchen.

"And just for the record"—he opened the oven—"I don't mind giving you rides. You can at least let me help you that way."

"All right." I rubbed my tummy. "That smell is making me hungry."

"Perfect because it's time to eat." He carried the dish to the table. "And, Cami, thank you for telling me."

"I didn't want to send you running for the hills."

He pulled out a chair for me to sit down. "I'm enjoying getting to know you. And so far, I like what I see. All of it."

This was the type of positive energy I needed in my life.

CHAPTER 11

Popping into Tessa's shop each morning was more than a habit. It was a necessity.

"Just coffee today. If I keep eating doughnuts every morning, I won't fit in that tiny apartment anymore." I sat down at the table closest to the counter.

Tessa laughed. "How dare you call my doughnuts fattening."

"Sorry. So, once Delany gets here, I'll tell you all about why I was crying and why there are boxes in my apartment waiting to be packed."

Tessa slapped a hand to her mouth. "You can't move."

"You're moving?" Delaney rushed up to the table.

"You should add a squeak to that door or a bell maybe. And, no, I'm not moving. My parents want me to move home. To motivate me, they threatened to take away all my stuff… my car, my designer clothes, my phone. They can have it. I'm not moving. Know of any good places to get affordable clothes?"

Delaney grinned. "Oh girl, I'll take you to all the best

resale shops around. And getting a phone shouldn't cost you too much. You can do this."

"And we can help when you need a ride. Until you can afford to get your own car."

I clapped. "I'm excited. At first, I wasn't sure what to do, and I came really close to telling my daddy I'd move back home, but I can't do that. It's time for me to figure things out on my own. And I'm just saying no to their money. They'll still be my parents. They'll still love me." Saying it out loud didn't make it feel more true.

"Why would you move away from a guy like Harper?" Delaney poked my arm.

"Right? He can cook!" My outlook was bright. "I need to run. I don't want Nacha and Haley panicking when they see the boxes."

"I'm glad you're okay." Tessa refilled my coffee cup. "And that you aren't moving."

"Me too." Delaney patted my hand.

"Me three." I hurried back to the studio and walked in just ahead of Nacha and Haley. I was waiting when they stepped in. "I'm not moving. Don't let the boxes give you the wrong idea. I'm just getting rid of some stuff."

"Getting rid of some stuff?" Haley pulled her curls up and looped a scrunchie around them.

"Anything my parents paid for. But I promise to wear clothes to work."

Nacha rolled her eyes. "If you need help…"

"I don't. Really. I'll figure it out." I wasn't sure how, but I was determined.

* * *

I HADN'T TALKED to my parents since that night at dinner. But with only two days until the big deadline, it was time to let

Daddy know I wouldn't be going home. Staring at the phone didn't help me figure out how to start the conversation.

Then I decided that the conversation needed to take place face-to-face. And if I'd been wrong about the whole still-loving-me part, it could be my last opportunity to go home.

I shoved a few things in an overnight bag. With the right puzzling skills, all the boxes would fit in my vehicle.

When Harper called, I tossed my bag aside. "Hey there, handsome."

"Hello to you too. I'm going to say this quick just in case I have to dart away. I'm thinking about visiting a friend in Houston this weekend."

"Is this an offer to drive me home if I decide to drop my stuff off in person?"

"Yes, ma'am." His added Southern twang was intoxicating.

"When you say it like that, I get this urgent desire to see you in a cowboy hat."

"I'll see what I can do."

"And thank you. I think it would be good to take my stuff home. Who knows when I'll be invited back again."

"When will you head over there?"

"I'll leave in the morning. Not too early because I'll have to pack my car first. I was planning to spend the night."

He sighed when noises sounded in the background. "I'll stop by when I get off. And staying the night is fine. Bye."

Instead of calling my parents, I shot off a text to them, using the phone I hadn't used in over a week. *Driving to Houston tomorrow. Will text when I'm leaving.* After sending the message, I turned off the phone.

They were probably giddy, and I felt a little guilty about that. If they knew what my answer was going to be, they might have told me not to come. And I needed to give them the answer in person. That had to be worth points on the final exam.

My apartment didn't feel quite as tiny with half my stuff missing. But the cute clothes hanging on the bar were all items that I'd paid for with my money. Except the costume. That particular item had sentimental value.

My sense of accomplishment boosted my optimism about how the weekend would go.

* * *

Harper showed up bright and early with my favorite doughnut and a hot cup of coffee. "I'll load your car while you have breakfast."

"I'm nervous."

"I know." He squeezed my hand. "You can do this. And when you're ready to come home, text me, and I'll be there to pick you up as soon as I can."

"In Houston, that could be two hours, depending on where your friend lives."

"I lied about the friend part." He crinkled his nose. "Can you forgive me?"

"You are driving all that way—"

"To be sure you make it home safely. And I want to be there for you if you need me."

I turned around and ran up the short hall.

"Where are you going? Did I say something wrong?" Harper sounded a bit panicked as he chased after me.

"I just needed a place to put my coffee down. And my doughnut. So I could do this." I threw my arms around his neck.

Laughter rumbled in his chest as his lips met mine. He made it easy to be optimistic.

He had my SUV loaded soon after I finished my coffee. "You're all packed."

"I sent you the address to a coffee place. It's close to my

house. Let's meet there." I gave him a quick peck before sliding behind the wheel. "And thank you for making the trip."

He nodded, then closed my door.

* * *

Hours alone in the car undid every shred of optimism. And now that I was almost home, I was extra glad Harper had made the trip.

Knowing he was in town made it easier not to give into what my daddy wanted. Far away, I had oodles of determination. At home, I felt like a kid again.

I pulled into the coffee shop, and Harper parked beside me.

Climbing into his passenger seat, I focused on taking even breaths. "This is probably a good place for you to stop following me." I texted him my address. "My house isn't far from here. I'll update you soon."

He rested an open hand on the center console.

I slipped my fingers into his hand. "I'm happy you came with me. Super happy about that." After a quick kiss, I jumped out and got back into my car.

He waved as I backed out of my parking space.

A horn blared, and I slammed on the brakes. Crashing my car now would be the worst.

After waiting for the five hundred cars to go by—it only felt that way—I backed out and headed home. I reminded myself not to hold my breath all the way there.

CHAPTER 12

When I parked in the driveway, I grabbed anything I wasn't leaving behind. My silent pep talk about growing up helped me make it to the door.

Daddy opened it, a wide smile on his face. "You came to your senses."

"I did, but not in the way you think. I'm not staying."

His jaw clenched, and anger flared in his eyes. His reaction made the next part harder to say.

There was no way I was changing my mind now. "It's time I grew up, and you're right. It's not fair for me to take your money. I should be able to pay my own way. And I plan to do that."

"You came all this way to tell me that?"

"You deserved a face-to-face answer." I might've needed this more than he did. I handed him my keys and phone. "Stuff is boxed up and in the car. And there is some furniture and a few other things in a storage unit in San Antonio. It wouldn't fit in the vehicle."

Mom walked toward the door. "Is Camille here?"

Dad turned around. "Yes, but she's not staying. Want to say goodbye?"

"Goodbye? Why isn't she staying?" She paled. "What happened?"

After a deep breath, I plastered on the requisite smile. "I just came by to drop off the SUV and my stuff." I hugged her like I might never see her again. "Love you, Mom."

The tears in her eyes summed up how I felt.

I even hugged my dad. "Thanks, Dad. I'll send you the details about the storage unit. The key is on the ring."

He might not have noticed the change, but I'd chosen my words intentionally. I was no longer Daddy's little girl.

To say that my heart wasn't breaking would be a lie. Saying no to their money meant I wasn't invited inside. This wasn't love.

But I could get through this. "I'm going to go ahead and go. Bye." Rather than waiting in the front yard for Harper to drive over, I headed down the driveway toward the street. I'd just let Mom and Dad wonder how I planned to get home.

And I'm sure that was exactly what they were wondering as they stared at me. Why did the driveway have to be so long? It took forever to make it to the street. And even then, I wasn't out of sight until I reached the end of the block.

Once there, I called Harper.

He answered right away. "I didn't expect to hear from you so soon."

"Yep. It went *that* well. I'm walking to the coffee shop. You can just wait for me." I hung up before I got emotional.

When I turned the corner, it started to rain. It was as if someone had scripted the sad movie sequence for my life.

A car sped by, splashing me with water from the street. I wasn't going to ask how things could get worse.

The same car backed up and stopped along the curb. The guy got out, and I broke into a run.

"Cami! What are you doing over here?" Chase called out. "I was on my way to see you."

Even Mom and Dad couldn't agree on what was best for me.

Chase jumped back into his fancy sports car, something newer than I'd seen him driving before, and whipped the car around. Running faster wasn't going to solve this. No matter how much determination I had, I couldn't outrun a sportscar. Any car for that matter.

I stopped at the corner to avoid being hit by a soccer mom in an oversized SUV, and Chase stopped his car in the middle of the street.

He grabbed my arm before I could dart away. "What's going on with you? Do you need a ride?"

"I don't. Thank you." I shook my arm, wanting him to let go.

He didn't. "You act like you aren't happy to see me."

"Smart man. Very observant." I adjusted the overnight bag on my arm to keep it from slipping.

A truck pulled up to the curb, and as the door swung open, I swung the bag at Chase's chest.

Shocked, he let go of me.

"Bye." I ran to the truck and climbed in before Harper made it to the sidewalk. He turned around and hopped back into the driver's seat.

Chase gaped as we drove away.

"That was my ex. He's a bit full of himself." I buckled my seat belt, then tossed my bag into the back seat.

Harper blew out a breath. "His mouth was about to be full of my fist."

"Not worth it." I slouched in the seat. "I'm a mess."

"You can cry if you need to. I totally understand."

"I meant a literal mess. My clothes are soaked, and thanks to Chase, I have mud splattered all over my jeans."

I rubbed Harper's arm. "Thank you for coming to get me."

"I was trying to save you from the rain."

I hoped he didn't get tired of saving me. So far, he was doing it a lot.

"What do you say we find a place to eat? I'll buy you lunch, and you can change clothes in the bathroom."

"Sounds great." My new chapter had started, and the tears I'd expected never came. Adrenaline from being accosted by Chase had changed all that.

I'd never seen Harper so mad. And I'd never been happier to be rescued.

* * *

Something brushed my cheek, and my eyes sprang open. "Where are we?"

Harper smiled. "We're home."

"I didn't mean to fall asleep." I wiped at a tickle on my cheek.

"You were crying in your sleep." Harper tapped the steering wheel. "It was torturous."

"I'm sorry."

"You aren't the one who should apologize." He kissed my hand. "I'll carry your bag in for you. I've seen what you can do with it."

Laughing, I clasped his hand. "Thank you for everything today. And I'm not as torn up as I thought I'd be."

"Good. Want to come over? I'll order a pizza."

"That sounds great."

He kissed my hand and shifted into gear. "Eli might be there."

"I'll be nice."

Laughing, Harper shook his head. "When you climbed

into the truck after whapping Chase, you were the same Cami who'd hugged me on the sidewalk and again by the pool. The woman who slid down the bowling lane was different. I didn't dislike the other version of Cami, but this feels like the real you."

"I hadn't really thought about how different I was when my parents were around or otherwise inserted into my life."

He pinched his lips together. "Let's go eat."

There was something he hadn't said, but I didn't think it was a prelude to goodbye. And if it was, I didn't want to hear it right now.

CHAPTER 13

By the middle of the week, I couldn't muster any optimism. There wasn't enough work to keep me busy. I hadn't been called for a modeling job in weeks. And my apartment felt smaller by the day.

The only upside was the social media work I was doing. I only helped out friends, and I wasn't getting compensation for it. That wasn't going to pay my bills.

My hope that I'd find a great and grown-up solution withered.

I paced in the studio when the phones were quiet. Maybe the exercise would ignite a genius thought.

Haley leaned out of her office. "Go grab a doughnut. The back and forth is making me crazy."

Or maybe not.

I grabbed my purse. "Text me if you need anything."

The shop was quiet. The midmorning lull was a great time to talk to Tessa.

"Coffee?" Tessa held up a mug.

"No. I've had four already. That's a bad idea when I'm this

stressed." With my back facing the counter, I dropped into a chair.

"No leads on a different job?" She sat down across from me at a table.

"Nothing. You and Delaney make it look so easy! You have businesses. I can't even find a decent place to live on what I make."

The door opened, and Tessa jumped up. "How can I help you?"

"It'll take me a minute to decide. I'll let you know when I'm ready to order," a woman said.

Not all customers were as nice.

As soon as Tessa sat down again, I continued, "I love working there, but I need another job and a different place to live. I don't even have a car anymore. What am I going to do?" Mostly, I was venting. I knew Tessa didn't have the solution.

A hand touched my shoulder. "Forgive me for eavesdropping, but—"

I gasped when I turned around. "You're Haley's aunt! Please don't tell them what you heard. I haven't mentioned anything about trying to find a second job. They are not being greedy. It's not that at all. In fact, I think me working full-time is making it tight for them because Nacha is working fewer hours some days because of the baby. But you probably know about the baby."

The woman grinned. "Yep. And I'm more than a little excited. What kind of job are you wanting?"

This was what caused me the most trouble. I knew what I didn't want to do. Anything else—almost anything else—I'd be willing to try. "Not sure really. I'm open to all possibilities. The only things scratched off my list are working in fast food —because I was repeatedly told I wasn't good at it—and being an engineer. I hated that job. But I was good at it. Doesn't seem at all fair." I'd rambled long enough.

"Well, I have a goat farm and could use some extra help. There is also a trailer on the property if you'd like to live there."

Goats? I'd never thought of myself as an outdoorsy sort of girl, and I'd have put being a spy as a higher possibility than working with farm animals. But life was funny that way. "I don't know anything about goats. Except that they say 'Bah, bah.' That's what they say, right?"

"Something like that. And I'll teach you how to care for them. Someone has been teaching me. He still comes around, and I'll never complain about that. If you know what I mean." The woman winked.

I was quite sure I didn't want to know.

"Transportation would be kind of an issue. I don't have a car."

She rubbed my arm. "We can work something out. And if you wanted to continue working at the studio part-time, that wouldn't be a problem. Here's my number. If you want the job, call me. I can bring my truck and help you move."

My head spun like a ceiling fan on high speed. "When would I start?"

"As soon as you want."

I picked up the napkin where she'd written her number. "Thank you. I'm Cami, by the way. I know we've met but I wasn't sure if you remembered my name." I was hoping she'd tell me hers because I always called her Haley's aunt. I didn't know her actual name.

"Joji." She turned to Tessa. "I'm ready to order. I'll take one of everything in the case. That'll surprise my cowboy."

Tessa was having a good day, and so was I. I couldn't wait to talk to Haley and Nacha. That was next on my to-do list.

After Joji left with her huge order, I hugged Tessa, then ran next door.

"Haley, could I talk to you and Nacha about something? It won't take long."

Nacha walked out of her office. The sleeve of crackers in her hand was almost a permanent fixture. "What's going on?"

"If there is anything we can do to help you, we'll do all we can." Haley perched on the edge of my desk.

"We all know that some days there just isn't enough to keep me busy all day. And while I appreciate being able to live in that apartment, I really need more space. And a kitchen. Not that I cook, but still. Anyway, would y'all be okay with me going back to part-time? Like when I first started?"

Nacha teared up as she nodded. "That would be great."

Haley's shoulders relaxed. "We'd be one hundred percent on board with that."

"Good. Because I'm taking a second job. And I'm moving."

"Where?" Both ladies asked in unison.

"Your Aunt Joji asked me to work at the goat farm. And she said I could live in the trailer there. I'll have my own place and two real jobs. I need to call her and sort out the details. But I think this is good for me." I couldn't wait to tell Harper all about this recent turn of events.

Haley laughed. "Sorry. I was picturing you with goats. But I think it's great. Look at you! You don't need your dad's money."

It was silly to have a squad of people cheering me on for growing up, but I loved it. "Thanks, y'all. None of this would have happened without the two of you. I even met Harper because of you."

Nacha wiped her eyes. "I'm happy for you, Cami. Really and truly delighted for you."

My phone buzzed, and I checked my messages. "Harper wants to take me to lunch."

"Have fun. And you might not mention to Harper that there are cowboys coming and going on Aunt Joji's goat farm." Haley waved as she walked back into her office.

Not long ago, having cowboys around would have been a huge plus for taking the job. Now, I didn't care. I had eyes for one guy. And he was taking me to lunch.

CHAPTER 14

I took a picture of the tray loaded with barbecue. "I want to post this."

Harper grinned. "Are you doing their social media now too?"

"Oh, no. I want it for my page." I wasn't going to hide anymore, afraid of what my parents would think of my choices.

I typed out the caption—*Barbecue + my superhero = The perfect lunch date*—and showed him before posting. "See."

"Fabulous." He winked. That word had been added to his vocabulary because of me.

"I enjoy this. You can plan on me taking a lot more pictures."

"Fine with me. How long are you going to make me wait to hear your good news?"

I nudged the tray toward him. "You are looking at the newest farm girl at Joji's place."

His eyes widened. "A farm?"

Nodding, I laughed. "A goat farm."

"Real goats?"

"Yep. And the even better part, there's a trailer on the property, and I can live there. I still need to call her and work out the fine print. But I'm excited. And… I almost forgot. I'll still be working at the studio part-time."

"It seems perfect." He pointed at the food. "Are you going to eat?"

"Yes! I'm starved. Good news makes me hungry." I picked up a rib. "How's your day?"

"Better now. Adam and Eve invited us for dinner tonight. I'm not sure if you're up for that. I know it's last minute."

"Fun. Yes. Absolutely. Their baby is due any day, isn't it?"

"Sure is."

I'd met Adam and Eve and seen them at parties, but we hadn't gotten together with just them. And it felt a little monumental because Adam and Harper were close friends. Having dinner with his friends made us feel more like a couple. And I loved that.

"Do you miss not working with Adam?"

"I do. That was the biggest downside to moving out here. Especially because I don't see him nearly as often now that he's married."

"Well, I'm glad they invited us. I'm looking forward to it."

"Me too. When are you going to talk to Joji?"

"Whenever I get a few quiet minutes at work." I grabbed his hand. "I'm so excited. Working on a goat farm is definitely something I haven't tried before."

"Choosing your own adventure looks good on you." He listened, then used my words to compliment me later.

I snapped a picture of his smiling face but didn't post it.

If my parents did find my page, they could see my barbecue lunch, my morning doughnuts, my coffee, and even the goats.

But not Harper.

They'd get to see his face when they met him in person.

ONE CHOICE I'D NEVER MAKE

* * *

BETWEEN HAVING DINNER WITH FRIENDS, working, and posting on social media for my friends, I somehow managed to pack up my apartment in record time. I didn't have much, but it was all mine.

Everything I owned except two boxes fit into the bed of Joji's truck. The other two boxes were in the bed of Harper's truck.

Joji climbed into her monster of a pickup. "I'll meet you out there. You have the directions?"

"Got 'em." Harper draped an arm around my shoulders. "We won't be far behind you."

I leaned into him as she drove away. "I can't believe I'm moving to a goat farm."

"It hasn't even been a week since you gave the stuff back, and now you have a new place to live and a second job." He pressed a kiss to my temple. "The goat farm bit surprised me too."

"I'm sure I'll learn a lot. Hopefully, I won't start smelling like a goat." That thought terrified me. "Let me double-check that I locked the door. Then we can go."

He caught my hand as I stepped away. The way he looked at me made my toes go numb.

"What?"

"Go check the door." He let my fingers slip out of his hand as I stepped away.

After pulling on the handle, I met him at the passenger door. "I'm ready for my new adventure."

One half of me was excited about the newness of it all. The other part was terrified of failing miserably.

Rather than open the door, Harper slipped an arm around my waist.

With my back against the side of the truck, I tilted my head, hoping for a whopper of a kiss.

Gently, he teased his lips on mine. I inched up, pressing into him. His fingers threaded into my hair, and if his arm hadn't been around me, I would've melted onto the pavement like chocolate in the summer sun.

I gasped when he pulled away. "Wow. What was that for?"

"For luck on your new adventure."

"I'm pretty sure I'm going to need lots of luck. Especially that kind of luck."

He winked as he opened the door. "I'm happy to accommodate you."

It took less than ten minutes to get to the farm, which was like icing on my cupcake. I'd found a second job and a place to live, and Harper was still close by.

"Thanks for all your help today. Joji said she'd ask some of the guys to help us unload."

"Which is why I'm happy I wasn't working today. So I could also be there to help."

I loved how funny he was.

"I'm probably crazy for moving to a place I haven't even seen, but how bad can it be? She said there was furniture."

"I doubt Haley's aunt would have offered the trailer if it weren't livable." Harper drove through the open gate.

I leaned forward in my seat. "This is the place. It's pretty much the middle of nowhere. Definitely different than the little strip mall in town."

I plastered on a smile as I climbed out of the truck. Adventure was great, but seeing the farm made it seem real in a terrifying way. I'd be taking care of goats. Goats smelled bad and ate whatever they could get their mouths on.

But braving new challenges was part of growing up.

* * *

JOJI STOOD in the living room with her hands on her hips. "That's pretty much it. As you can see, I left stuff up on the walls, but feel free to take it down. Isn't this picture just adorable though? This couple lived here before Beau bought the place. Any questions?"

There were so many questions bumping around in my head. "More than we have time for. When do I meet the animals?"

She laughed. "I love your enthusiasm."

"Right?" Harper kissed the top of my head. "I'll just wait here while Joji shows you around outside."

"Don't you want to meet the goats?" I bumped my hip against his.

"There will be plenty of time for that."

Joji stepped outside.

I turned to face him. "You'll stay until I get back, right?"

He nodded. "Of course. But this will give you and Joji time to talk."

I kissed his cheek before running out the door.

This was the part that made me the most nervous. Animals. And I wanted to get this first hurdle over with. Kind of like jumping into a pool to get over a small fear of water.

I could barely take care of myself, and Joji was trusting me with the lives of these four-legged creatures. And chickens. Chickens didn't fit in the four-legged category.

A big dog sauntered off Joji's porch and bumped my hand with his nose.

"That's Bones. He's new around here." Joji opened the barn door. "He seems to like you."

I scratched his head. "We can learn together. You going to help me, Bones?"

He wagged his tail.

"I've never had a dog before. Any pets actually. Mom

thought they were too messy. Actually that's not true. Not the part about Mom. She hated the idea. But she also has a phobia of cats. She thinks she's kept it a secret, but the one time I saw her around a cat, I knew. Anyway, all that to say, I did have a cat once. I managed to keep it in my room almost six weeks before the maid discovered my kitty. You can guess what happened when Mom found out. Bye, bye, cat."

"Around here, there are lots of cats. And before buying this place, I never had pets either. So you're in good company." Joji pointed at the stalls. "When we have babies separated from the nannies, we keep them in here, but we've just weaned the only two little ones, so they are out in the outdoor pens for now."

We continued through the barn and out the back door. Two pens held lots of goats.

"Guys and Gals." She pointed as she spoke. "Most days, I let the wethers roam. They keep the grass cut, but since I was out and about, I kept them in the pen."

Leaves rustled in the tree at the edge of the pen. "There's a goat in that tree! We should get him down."

She laughed. "It's tempting to let you climb up there. Especially since we have a fireman here to rescue you, but Boingo can get himself back to the ground all by himself. He jumps fences and climbs trees whenever he feels like it."

"I'm surprised he isn't out roaming."

"Boingo is social. He likes to be near his buddies, so he stays in the pen for the most part. Unless there is something interesting outside the pen. And that one over there is Bumpo. Never bend over when he's in the pen with you." Joji rubbed her backside. "Don't do it."

I backed away from that pen. "Noted."

"And another thing. Always close the gate when going in or out. I learned that lesson the hard way." She led me back through the barn. "Chickens are over there. Cats are kind of everywhere. Sometimes they sleep in the house, but lately, they've been out and about more."

"When do I start, you know, doing farm work?"

"In the morning. I do chores between six thirty and seven. If you want breakfast or coffee, just knock. I'm up by six every morning."

Six was early.

"Okay. Thanks."

"I'll take care of things tonight. You need time to settle in."

"And unpack. Labeling the boxes would've been a good idea. Too late for that now." Good ideas always came to me too late.

"See you in the morning." She waved as she walked onto her patio.

I scraped the dirt off my shoes before walking into my new place.

"How was it?" Harper leaned forward, his elbows resting on his knees.

"I learned that I'm going to need different shoes. My cute sandals are now a mess." I scanned the stacks of boxes. "Ugh. I don't even know where to start."

He reached behind the sofa and picked up a box wrapped in bright pink paper. The silver bow on the top had more loops than a Houston interchange. "A housewarming gift."

"You didn't have to get me anything. But thank you." I tore away the paper. As soon as I saw the corner of the box, I threw my arms around him and kissed him.

Laughing, he lifted me off my feet. "I knew you loved coffee. I just didn't realize how much."

"I don't have a coffee maker. I always got coffee at Tessa's. And Joji said I could get coffee at her house, but I don't want to have to get dressed before coffee. I mean, I do now, but at my own place, I want to drink coffee without caring how I look." I gave him another quick peck. "This is the perfect gift."

"I'm glad you like it. Now, show me what to unpack." He rubbed his hands together.

I finished unwrapping my new coffee maker. "I think this will look perfect on the counter there in the corner. Oh, when I told Joji that I can't cook, that is true, but I'm open to learning. I probably need lessons."

"Cooking lessons?"

"Yes. Private lessons. And if the teacher were also trained in putting out fires, that would be convenient."

Harper walked up behind me and wrapped his arms around me. "Why is that? Do you have plans to set the kitchen on fire?"

"No! That wasn't what I meant."

He laughed. "Then I assume you want me to teach you to cook."

"That's exactly what I want." I sighed. "Most people have all of this figured out by now."

He patted my hip. "Let's get some of these boxes unpacked."

I yanked scissors out of my purse. "I remembered not to pack these. It makes opening boxes easier."

Using the scissors, he opened the box on the top of a stack. "Smart. When I moved to Stadtburg, I was using a key to get boxes open until I found my pocketknife buried in a box where it didn't belong." He peeked into the box. "And this one goes to the bedroom. I'll let you take care of unpacking the contents of this."

The way I'd tossed my bras and panties on the top of other clothes made it look like intimates filled the entire box.

Giggling, I sliced the tape on the top of another box. "You make me laugh."

"That's a plus, right?"

"A huge plus."

Working side by side, we unpacked nearly half the boxes.

"That's enough for tonight. I have sheets for the bed, and I can find clothes. We should grab dinner."

"Good plan." He stopped before pushing open the door. "Grab those keys Joji gave you. We'll take your new wheels."

"Are you sure? That purple monster is huge."

He tucked an arm around my waist. "It'll be fun. You'll drive."

Goat farming seemed easy compared to the idea of driving that truck.

"Today is as good a day as any. Let's hope I don't run over anything important."

Harper laughed. "I vote for just not running over anything at all."

I climbed up and buckled into the driver's seat.

Once Harper was secured in his seat, I shifted into reverse. The rumble of the engine was oddly empowering.

"Ready or not, here I go."

His knuckles were only a tad white from gripping the door handle. He trusted me.

I backed up, then drove toward the road. Thankfully, this stretch of the road seemed quiet. As I turned right, the truck rolled over something with its back tire.

"That wasn't a person, was it?" I craned my neck, scanning the pavement behind me.

"It was a rock. And you are almost off the road on this side."

I hugged the center line a bit more. "I have to get used to the size, but wow. I sort of like this."

"Do you?"

"It makes me feel powerful." I turned to face him. "It's exhilarating."

"Keep your eyes on the road." He squeezed my arm. "And

this suits you. Didn't think so when I first saw it. But I do now."

I grinned at him, then looked back out at the road. "It does suit me."

The cloud of quiet worry about what my parents would think didn't weigh on me like before. I knew what they'd think of the truck, the farm, and the trailer.

They'd hate all of it. And I'd be sure to post about those things in case they were stalking my page.

The only one of my choices they wouldn't hate was Harper.

But I had to wait a while before introducing him. I needed them to see that I had a handle on my independence.

CHAPTER 15

The sun was still asleep when I crawled out of bed. I'd only snoozed my alarm once. Wearing my cute discount-store pajamas and with my hair piled on top of my head in an unattractive knot, I padded down the hall to the kitchen.

I'd prepped the coffee maker last night, and the beep on the machine was why I hadn't snoozed a second time. Amazing goodness awaited me.

When I opened the cabinet, the notecard sticking up out of one of the mugs caught my attention.

The handwritten note put a huge smile on my face.

Morning, beautiful. I hope your day is fabulous.

Either Harper had been extra sneaky and left me this sweet note, or some creepy person had snuck into the trailer while I was sleeping.

I preferred to think that Harper had left me the note.

He was probably awake by now. His shift at the fire station started in less than an hour.

I shot off a text. *Love the note.*

A kissing emoji was his reply.

After pouring my coffee, I sent one more text. *Thanks for the good luck.*

He didn't answer. Surely, he got my reference to his kiss for luck.

I stared at my phone as I drank my coffee, waiting for a response.

Had I come on too strong?

He was the one who'd left the note.

Maybe using the L-word had scared him off. But I hadn't said I loved him. Just the note.

Or maybe he was just doing adult things like eating breakfast, or fixing his bed, or showering before work. I needed to stop thinking about what he was doing.

What I needed to do was start getting dressed. It was a quarter past six, and I was nowhere near presentable.

After downing the last of my coffee, I poured myself a second cup. The first one helped me wake up. The second one would hopefully drown my disappointment that Harper hadn't messaged back.

My mug was almost to my lips when a knock sounded, and I ended up with coffee dribbled down the front of me. Focused on wiping the front of my jammies, I pulled open the door. "Joji, give me two minutes, and I'll be ready to do chores." I glanced up as I said the last word.

"Thought you might need a doughnut with sprinkles to go with your coffee." Harper held out a little white bag. "And maybe a little luck."

"I don't know whether to kiss you or run and hide. I look awful."

"Want my vote?"

"Come in. Help yourself to coffee while I throw on real clothes." I handed him my coffee before running down the hall. "Don't drink mine. The cups are in the cabinet."

He called out, "Don't be too long. I can only stay for a few minutes."

I yanked on a cute top and my overalls. That was the perfect uniform for a farm job, right? There wasn't enough time to do anything with my hair.

"Ta-da!" I struck a pose when I hit the end of the hall. "I was fast. Just don't look at my hair. Now, where's my luck?" Kissing Harper was way more important than the doughnut, and admitting that out loud would hopefully not send him running. But just in case, I didn't say that out loud.

"You look amazing. The goats will be impressed." He took his time crossing the room, but he never broke eye contact. "I am."

I could feel heat flooding my cheeks, and I wasn't typically a blusher. "Tessa and Delaney went shopping with me, and we found lots of great stuff—"

Getting cut off with a kiss didn't bother me in the least.

When he stepped back, I fell forward. He caught me because he was the type to save people.

"I'd love to stay longer, but I need to run." He didn't move.

I slipped my arms around his waist. "Thank you for this surprise."

He smiled, then kissed the top of my head. "I really need to go. And your jammies are cute, by the way." Laughing, he strolled out the door.

Not moving back to Houston was the best decision I'd ever made. Breaking off my engagement to Chase was a close second.

Wrong.

Hugging Harper on the sidewalk was the best decision I'd ever made. I couldn't imagine anyone more perfect for me.

* * *

Joji stood in the middle of the barn with her hands on her hips. "So, you know how to feed the chickens and to watch out for the red one with the bad attitude. You know about collecting the eggs and where to put them. We talked about feeding the goats." She danced her eyebrows. "Ready to milk a goat?"

"I was born ready." Not in the least, but it didn't really matter.

She prepped the stand, explaining what was needed and how it would be used. I prayed that she'd give me another lesson before I had to do this by myself.

"So, the goats get a special treat while you milk them?" I watched over her shoulder as she dumped a cup of goat food-type stuff into the mini trough.

"It keeps them happy. Let me grab Maude. We'll start with her because she's usually polite."

"That sounds worrisome."

Joji laughed as she walked out of the barn. "It'll be fine."

A minute later, the goat was in the contraption, happily eating the goodies.

"First, we clean her off with this rag and bucket. Then we waste a squirt. I use this pan. And now we are ready for milking. You want to squeeze it. Don't pull on it." Joji stood up and pointed at the milking stool. "Have a seat and give it a try."

I was glad there was no one filming me. But if ever something was social media worthy, this was it.

After pushing my sleeves up near my elbows, I inhaled. "Hello, Maude. My name is Cami. I'm going to, um, milk you. Soooo, I need to grab your teat. Actually teats, plural. Please don't be mad."

Joji's giggling didn't make any of this easier.

I reached out my hand but pulled back before touching

Maude. "What does it feel like? Is it firm or squishy? Never mind."

Maude shifted, and I jumped back.

"She's going to run out of treats." Joji's shoulders were still bouncing.

"Right. Okay. Here goes." I grabbed one teat and squeezed. Liquid hit me in the knee, and I launched away from the milking stand. "I sprayed myself."

Joji bent over, and I worried she wasn't getting enough air.

"Are you okay?"

Her head bobbed up and down, and she grabbed her stomach. "Yes, sorry. You make me laugh."

"We could've charged admission for people to watch." I dropped back onto the stool, determined to get milk into the bucket. "Now that I can get the milk to come out, I just need to work on my aim."

"Give it another try." Joji backed up a bit.

I grinned when milk splattered against the inside of the bucket. "I did it. I'm milking a goat."

No one would accuse me of being fast or efficient. I still jumped every time Maude moved and occasionally landed milk outside the bucket. But on day one, I was milking a goat.

"You did a great job. Let me grab the next one. I always milk them in the same order. It's easier that way. They like the routine."

One more thing to remember.

"When we're done with milking, you can take a short break. Then Clint is going to come show you how to muck the stalls."

"Is he the big guy who doesn't smile much?"

She grinned. "Yep. I'd teach you, but I have cheese I need to make. And he volunteered."

I had a feeling he wasn't going to giggle about my antics like Joji did.

* * *

Clint was about as warm as an iceberg and just about as big. "Here put this on."

A bandana?

My messy bun was a little extra messy, but was it really so bad that he didn't want to look at it? I folded the bandana into a triangle, then tied it around my head. I needed a mirror to know how it looked, but since the barn didn't have one, my phone would have to suffice.

Cameras couldn't lie. Filters were an entirely different story. But even without a filter, I looked pretty good.

Then Clint laughed. He knew exactly how to give a girl a complex.

"What? Is it crooked? Is my hair—" That's when I noticed the bandana covering his face. "Oh. Like that."

I pulled the bright red bandana out of my hair, making a mental note to get some because I liked the look. It went well with my overalls.

Once I had my face covered, I picked up a shovel. "Now I'm ready."

"Joji was right about you. You're funny." Even behind the mask, his smile was obvious. His gaze dropped to my feet. "You are definitely going to need different shoes to do this."

"I have some rain boot-type things that my grandmother gave me a few years ago. They come up to just below the knee and have this adorable flower pattern all over them."

"Those'll work."

I dropped the shovel and ran to the trailer. Had I unpacked those boots? I smiled up at the sky. "Granny, I'm going to use the boots you gave me."

What would she have thought about my new adventure? She would have cheered me on. Rocking the boat was her favorite pastime. That was one reason I missed her so much.

When I stomped back into the barn, Clint had already started working.

"Tell me what to do." I grabbed the shovel.

He pointed at the yucky hay all over the floor. "Scoop up that and put it in the pile out there."

I stabbed my shovel into the hay and dropped at least half on the way to the pile.

"It's easier if you get it *all* in the pile."

"I'm trying." My next attempt was better. "I just need practice."

He watched more than he shoveled, probably so I'd get more practice.

"So, you and Joji, are y'all like a thing?" I'd seen the way he looked at her, but I didn't want to assume.

"A what?"

"You know, an item. Or do people like you still call it going steady?"

His brow pinched, and I was fairly certain there was no smile hiding behind the mask.

"We're friends."

"Yikes. You make it sound like a disease. She's cute, though, don't you think?"

He grunted, but I knew he meant yes. I had my work cut out for me here on the farm. Not only did the animals need my help, the people did too.

And I was up to the challenge.

Besides, if it worked out between them, I could add matchmaker to my resume.

CHAPTER 16

I sank into the couch, the most thankful I've ever been for the weekend. And I wasn't naïve enough to think work on the farm only happened on the weekdays, but Joji had told me to take the weekend off. And I didn't argue.

Now I understood why she didn't bother locking her door. When people came over, I was too tired to get up.

Starting next week, I'd be working afternoons at the studio Monday through Thursday. Just thinking about it made me tired.

This past week, I was up earlier and worked harder than I ever had before. I enjoyed it more than I expected, but my body was still adjusting.

"It's open." If my insides weren't begging for food, I'd go to bed even though it was only seven.

Tessa stepped in, and Delaney followed.

They set bags on the counter.

"Before I get distracted, who is the shirtless guy working out there?" Tessa peeked out the window.

"That's Tyler. He is a ranch hand at the place on the other side of the fence. He only comes over so he can see the yoga instructor when they have goat yoga. I'm not sure why he's out there working tonight."

"Goat yoga?" Delaney laughed and peeked out the window. "Does he have any friends?"

"There are a few who come around. All of them are built like that." I stretched. "Not that I've noticed or anything."

Tessa laid out vegetables and other packages on the counter. "You're blinded by love. How many mornings has Harper surprised you?"

"Only twice." I waited for the retort.

"And you've been here four days. That's a lot. Where are your pans?" Tessa opened cabinets. "Either a skillet or a sauté pan will work." She talked about pans like men talked about screwdrivers.

How was I supposed to know what she needed? "Let me run and ask Joji if we can borrow a pan. We only need the one?"

"And a pot for the rice. You seriously don't have pans?" She continued looking through cabinets.

"At my first place, my roommate had pans, so I didn't bother buying any. Then I lived with Nacha. Her kitchen was a dream, and I cooked a little when I was there. And the apartment in the studio didn't have a kitchen. And half of what I did have, I packed up and sent back to my parents." I pushed up off the couch.

She held up a folded notecard. "What's this? It was in your cabinet."

I snatched it out of her hand. "Not sure."

Harper had left me another note. *Thinking about you makes me smile. And I smile a lot.*

I stuck it in my pocket. "Harper left me a note."

Delaney furrowed her brow. "Let us know when he does

something wrong. I'm sort of waiting for that… just to rule out the possibility that he's a robot."

Rolling my eyes, I opened the front door. "Be right back."

Outside, I shot off a text to Harper. *How many notes did you leave in my house?*

He sent a smiley emoji as an answer.

I like the surprise of finding them.

Good. Enjoy your girls' night.

Thanks. I'll call you tomorrow morning. Late. I'm going to sleep in. I had grand plans for sleeping until well after the sun was up.

Sounds good.

Clint's truck was parked outside Joji's house, so I made sure I knocked. I didn't want to walk in and see something I couldn't unsee.

Clint opened the door. "Hello, Cami."

"Hi. Is Joji here?"

"Yes." He pointed toward the kitchen.

Wiping her hands on a dishtowel, Joji walked up to the door. "What's up, darling? Need something?"

"Um, if I'm interrupting something, I can come back another time." I probably should've kept my mouth shut about that, but the words popped out before I thought it through.

Clint walked away from the door.

That probably meant I was interrupting.

"No, not at all. I was just—doesn't matter. What do you need?" Joji draped the dish towel over her shoulder.

"My friends came over, and we were going to make dinner because I have a kitchen now. But I forgot to tell them that I didn't have any pots and pans."

She motioned for me to follow her. "I have extras. No pots and pans?"

"Not everyone needs them." Clint leaned on the counter.

"Exactly." I shoved my hands in my pockets. "Thanks, Clint."

He gave a slight nod. Saying two full sentences was too much to expect from the man.

Joji opened a cabinet and stuck her head in. "What are you cooking?"

"Rice. And chicken, I think. Maybe veggies."

She set three pans on the counter. "This saucepan should work for the rice, and then here's a skillet and a sauté pan."

"Thanks. I'll bring them back clean." I loaded my arms with the cookware.

"Keep them as long as you need." Joji smiled as Clint opened the front door.

I really wasn't buying the whole "we're friends" bit.

When I got back to the trailer, I kicked on the door.

Delaney opened it. "You saved dinner."

"Joji had extras."

Tessa helped me get the pans to the counter. "And these are nice."

I dropped back to my spot on the couch. "Yeah. Joji isn't a regular goat farmer. I'm not trying to say that goat farmers are poor. But she has money. I'm a little confused about how she ended up here. But I know why she stays."

Delaney raised an eyebrow. "Why is that?"

"That cowboy."

"The one in the garden?" She peeked out the blinds like Tessa had done earlier.

"Not that one. The old guy who taught me how to muck a stall. And trust me. You don't want to learn." I held up my hands. "You can't even tell that I've ever had a manicure. My cuticles are awful."

"You going to quit?" Tessa looked up, but the knife in her hand continued to move.

"Not a chance. And please don't cut off a finger." I walked to the counter, figuring I'd learn more about cooking if I were actually in the kitchen. "Tell me what you're doing."

"First, tell me more about Harper. Why are we here tonight and not the guy who can't go more than two days without seeing you?"

"He didn't even ask about coming over. Granted, when he showed up yesterday morning, the first thing I told him was that y'all were coming over. So, that's probably why."

She poured rice into a pan, then added water. "I'm glad you still want to spend time with us."

"It's a tough choice." I picked up a green bean and snapped off the end, mimicking what she'd started doing. "You know I'm joking, but seriously, I'm a little surprised he didn't run the other way. I'm not at my best right now, hovering somewhere between a spoiled child and an adult."

"You're making a lot of tough choices lately." Tessa tossed all the green beans into one of the pans.

"That's an understatement. I swore that I'd never do anything to make my dad this mad. I left my mom a message —just a hello, but still—she hasn't called me back. They've disowned me, and I hate it."

Delaney opened drawers until she found my wine bottle opener.

I didn't care who'd paid for it. Some things were needs, so I kept it.

"Give them time. Things will change, I bet." She poured wine into a glass. "Who else wants some?"

"Me! But only half a glass." I followed Tessa to the stove. "I hope so. I want them to meet Harper at some point. I think Mom and Dad will be impressed."

"Of course they will. He seems like a great guy." Tessa set the other pan on a burner, then turned down the temperature on the burner where the rice was cooking. "And I don't want to hear any more about how it's shocking that he likes you. You're likable. He'd be crazy not to."

I watched as she continued to cook, paying close attention and hoping she was right.

* * *

My blissful Saturday-morning sleep was interrupted by a screeching goat. Irritated, I yanked on my rain boots and stomped out to the barn in my pajamas.

When I got to the pen, I pointed at the noisy goat. "Shut up. Seriously. I'm trying to sleep. What is your problem?"

"She's in heat." Clint chuckled.

"Ugh. Can't you give her chocolate or something? Anything. I just want that noise to stop." I covered my ears and walked back to the trailer. Since sleep wasn't happening, I texted Harper. *Free today?*

Yep. I thought you were going to sleep in. He must've been near his phone because the message popped up right away.

Goats. That one word explained why I wasn't sleeping.

He sent a laughing emoji. I, however, wasn't ready to laugh about it.

Give me a half hour, and I'll be ready. I tossed my phone on the counter, then grabbed it again when my mom's picture popped up on the screen. "Mom, hi!"

"Hello, sweetheart. Thanks for calling the other day. I hope you know your dad and I still love you. We just want you to make wiser choices." She used her pacifying tone. Trying to keep everything peaceful at all costs was how my mom operated.

I swallowed my snotty response and tried a more adult approach. "I'm trying to make good choices, Mom. I can't depend on you and Dad for everything."

"I know you're trying. But I hope you know that you're welcome to change your mind about coming home. It's not like you've run off and married someone we hate. It can all be undone."

"I have a new job and a new place to live. It's bigger than my last place."

"Great news. Send me the new address. Is it an engineering job? We can ship your stuff back. We have it all stored in your room."

Why had I opened my big mouth? "It's not an engineering job."

"Oh. How are you? Really?" The façade slipped, and worry tinged Mom's question.

"Mom, I'm happy. At this job, I'm learning a bunch of new things, and I have great friends here in town. I know this isn't what you imagined for me, but I'm happy."

"Being happy now is fine, but we want you to think of the future. I need to run. Love you." She hung up without giving me a chance to respond.

Was she sneaking in a call to me when Dad wasn't around?

Probably.

I changed in a hurry, ready to do something—anything—to take my mind off that conversation.

Thankfully, when Harper knocked, I was no longer in my pajamas.

He held up grocery bags. "How about a cooking lesson?"

"Something yummy, I hope."

"Pancakes."

"Perfect." I picked up two of the pans. "Do we need the bigger one or the little one?"

"Probably the sauté pan."

I looked from one pan to the other. "The big one or the little one?"

"The big one."

Maybe now I could remember which was which.

I wouldn't say this to Tessa, but cooking with Harper was more fun. My opinion had probably been swayed by the added kisses for luck. And they worked. The pancakes were amazing.

"I'm almost too stuffed to move." Harper leaned back in his chair.

I carried the dishes to the sink. "They were so good."

"You did a great job. I'll help you clean up the kitchen, then we can go for a walk or a drive. Or even go back to my place and watch a movie."

I slipped my arms around his waist as he walked into the kitchen. "Any of those are fine. I just want to spend time with you." It was way too soon and I was way too broke to tell him I loved him, but I did. Or maybe I just loved the idea of him. Either way, I liked having him around. A lot.

He pulled me to his chest and held me a minute before speaking. "Let's go for a drive. But first, I want to meet the goats."

"That's right! I haven't introduced you. This'll be fun. I don't have all the names memorized yet, but I know which ones to watch out for."

A thump sounded on the porch, and Harper peeked out the door. "I'm guessing this one is on that list."

"Boingo, go back to your friends." I slipped out the door, blocking that silly goat from running inside. "He keeps coming over to my trailer. I don't know what his problem is."

"He likes you." Harper followed me out and pulled the door closed.

"Dishes can wait. I'll show you around now."

Tapping my leg, I walked toward the barn, and Boingo followed like he was a pet.

Then without help, I managed to get that goat back into his pen.

I wasn't bad at this.

CHAPTER 17

*A*fter weeks of working afternoons at the studio, my body finally adjusted to my new schedule. I no longer walked around looking like a zombie from two until bedtime, but most nights, I was asleep by ten. Before working on the farm, going to bed that early only happened when I was sick.

Tonight, Harper and I were watching a movie at his place. I really wanted to stay awake through the whole thing, so I brewed myself coffee.

I walked around the trailer, cleaning up so it didn't look like a slob lived here.

While I was on the floor, someone knocked.

"Come in."

Harper laughed as soon as the door swung open. "Looks like a pillow was attacked."

"It was." I picked up another handful of fluff. "Boingo destroyed my favorite pillow."

"You're letting him in the house now?"

"Let is not the word I'd use." I pointed at the trash can. "What's left of the pillow isn't even salvageable. I've been picking up fluff since then. Every time I think I have it all, more appears." I tossed the last few handfuls into the trash bag.

"I'll get you another pillow. Where'd you get it?"

"Chase gave it to me."

Harper's shoulders tensed, but only for a second. "I like Boingo. Have I mentioned that?"

"It was a nice pillow. And it wasn't as if he picked it out. His personal shopper did. She was great. The engagement ring she had designed was stunning."

Harper's eyes had never looked so green. "You ready to go?"

I crossed my arms. "I know you aren't jealous of some guy I whapped with my luggage. And do you know why I did that?"

"So he'd let go of your arm."

"I wanted him to let me go before you slugged him. And for the record, hitting him broke my favorite compact."

Harper fixed his gaze on me and blinked several times. "I might not have slugged him."

"I'm glad we didn't have to find out. Chase isn't a nice guy. And I have no doubt you could knock him out, but the legal trouble he'd rain down on you wouldn't be worth it." I inhaled, then let the breath out slowly, trying to calm down. "I love your green eyes, but not when they have that look in them."

The corners of his mouth twitched into a smile. "Tell me what you really think."

"I think you're twice the man Chase could ever hope to be." I turned and picked up my purse. "And gosh, I hope you never meet my old boss. He was worse."

"You know that cartoon where the little chicken whaps the big chicken with the hammer? That's the way I feel right now."

"It was a chicken hawk." I kissed him. "And I don't want those other guys."

He caught my hand and pulled me close. "Why is it that you can tell me what you think, but with your parents, you walk on eggshells?"

I was far too mentally exhausted to filter my answer. "Because I'm not afraid you'll walk away."

I'd probably said too much, and maybe he would walk away. I'd been wrong before.

He lifted my chin. "Cami, I'm sorry. I don't even know Chase, but after the way he was clutching your arm, I don't like him. And I also hope I never meet your old boss. When people hurt someone I care about, I can be a tad unforgiving. I'm not jealous of those guys. I'm mad at them."

I cupped one side of his face. "Don't be. That's just renting them space in your head, and they don't deserve it."

"Fair enough." He pressed his hand over mine. "I'm sorry about your pillow."

"Saying that first would've made this conversation a lot shorter." I gave him a quick peck. "But I'm glad we talked about it."

He nodded. "Me too."

I'd known him only a short time relative to how long I'd known my parents, and I trusted him not to leave me. I wasn't sure whether to cheer or cry. Harper cared about me. I knew he did.

What did that say about my parents?

* * *

THAT NIGHT AFTER DEVOURING A PIZZA, Harper and I snuggled on his sofa and watched a movie. Warm and content, I nestled closer to him and closed my eyes.

With him, I could pretend it didn't matter that my dad

hadn't called me back since I'd left him a message three weeks ago and that my mom made a point of sending me engagement announcements for every one of her friends' children.

Part of the reason I wanted them to call me was so I could have them meet Harper. I wanted them to see me happy. And he was a big part of that happiness.

He tucked an arm around me, and I gave up fighting sleep. He would have to wake me when the movie ended.

I wiped drool off my mouth as I opened my eyes. The house was dark, and I was alone on Harper's couch. I tossed back the quilt draped over me and followed the aroma of coffee.

Rubbing my eyes as I stepped into the kitchen, I asked, "Why are you having coffee so late?"

"Six in the morning isn't all that late." Eli didn't sound like a morning person.

I blinked. "Where's Harper?"

"Still asleep, I guess." He pointed at the mugs. "Big or small?"

"Big. Why didn't he wake me last night?"

Eli chuckled. "He tried. If this had been summer camp, you'd have woken up with your hair a different color or something. You were out cold."

"How embarrassing." I added sugar to my coffee, then nosed around the fridge for milk.

"Believe me, you have nothing to worry about. You could paint every wall in this house pink, and he'd try to find a reason to like it." Eli sipped his coffee. "If you get what I'm saying."

"I hope you're right." I jumped when the front door opened. "I guess he wasn't asleep."

I ran out to the living room.

Bare-chested, Harper was wiping his face with a T-shirt. "You're awake."

"Sorry I fell asleep on you. Literally." I tried to be nonchalant about drinking in the sight of his chest and six-pack.

"Didn't mind at all. Let me grab a quick shower, then I can run you home or take you to breakfast. Your choice." He started down the hall.

"Hey. No kiss hello?"

"I'm a sweaty mess."

I moved closer. "I don't care."

He grinned as he tossed his shirt aside.

Trailing a finger along a small scar on his shoulder, I asked, "What happened?"

"I fell out of a tree when I was a kid." He watched my finger move back and forth, then sucked in a breath when I pressed a kiss to the scar.

"You are a sweaty mess, but I still want you to kiss me."

Chuckling, he wrapped his arms around me and kissed me like we were the only two people in the whole wide world.

Behind me, Eli groaned. "I'm going back to bed."

I waved over my shoulder, hoping Eli was right about what he'd said during our little chat. I also wanted him to leave the room.

I preferred kissing without an audience.

CHAPTER 18

I walked out onto my porch and sat on the top step. Now that the evenings weren't as hot as blazes, I enjoyed being outside.

Eli's comment from last week played in my head. It was easy to believe he was right.

The only days I didn't see Harper were when he worked, but even on those days, he called me.

The part of me—the little girl inside—who felt unworthy of being loved liked to chatter on the days I didn't see him.

And I hated it. She could be quite convincing.

Boingo bleated before jumping the fence, then trotted up to me.

"Hey, buddy." I lifted up my phone. "Smile for me."

After snapping a picture of him, I posted it with the caption: *Hanging out with my second favorite fella*.

Within seconds, my favorite fella liked my post.

Boingo sat down next to me. He was a strange goat.

"What do you think, Boingo? Any advice for me?" I laughed after asking the question. "Maybe we need to create an advice column. People can send you questions. Let's see how you do. I'll start." I scratched behind his ear. "I have strong feelings for Harper. Well, because you're a goat and can't repeat this conversation, I'll come right out and say it—I love him. He hasn't used that word, though."

Boingo cocked his head.

"Be patient. I'm getting to my question." I was glad no one was around to see me having a heart-to-heart with a farm animal. "He's an amazing guy, and while I'm trying, I don't have a whole lot to offer. My own parents hardly speak to me. Should I break it off? Am I being unfair to him?"

That goat jumped up and bounded back into his pen.

"You're horrible at giving advice!" I was yelling at a goat.

"Want mine?" Joji walked around the end of the trailer. "I wasn't trying to eavesdrop, but I heard everything."

"You're like a feather floating around without making a sound." I flashed her a smile. "I'd love your advice."

She sat down next to me on the step. "It comes in two parts. One—you can't judge your lovability—we're going to pretend that's a real word or maybe it is." She shook her head. "Anyway, it isn't based on others. Sometimes broken people have a hard time with love. Some need time to heal. Other people just need a good slap, but that's a conversation for another time. Two—love is in the actions. Don't think it isn't there just because the word hasn't been used." She patted my hand. "Trust me. This is something I know through personal experience."

Clint drove up as if scripted into the scene.

She stood and waved. Before walking toward him, she turned back to me. "What action could you take that would say 'I love you'?"

I chased her down the stairs. "Wait! I need to hug you."

Laughing, she wrapped me in a tight embrace. The woman was tiny, but she gave the best bear hugs. "I love having you here."

ONE CHOICE I'D NEVER MAKE

"Tell Clint hello for me. I have an errand to run."

As I ran back to the trailer, Clint asked Joji, "What was that about?"

"She's in love." Joji had never been more right.

I'd have to see what I could do to help out her situation. But it would have to wait until later.

Right now, there was one place in town still open that served milkshakes.

With keys in hand, I climbed up into my truck.

I'd been so upset the day Harper had shown up with milkshakes. I remembered my chocolate one vividly, but what kind did he like?

By the time I made it to the counter, I had a plan. I ordered a chocolate and a vanilla, both topped with whipped cream and cherries. I'd drink whichever one he didn't want.

As I drove toward the station, I crossed my fingers that he wouldn't be out on a call.

When I parked my purple monster in the lot, one of the guys waved before walking inside. What was I supposed to do now? Should I just knock on the door?

Before I was even out of the truck, Harper came running out of the building, and his smile was the widest I'd ever seen it.

Whoever the other guy was, he knew who I was there to see.

Harper hugged me, then gave me a quick kiss. "Hey. What's up?"

I'd never shown up to the fire station before. And the elated expression on his face made me wish I hadn't waited so long to surprise him. "I was thinking about you, so I brought you a milkshake. But I couldn't remember if you liked vanilla or chocolate." I pointed toward the cup holders. "I bought one of each."

"Vanilla." He reached in and picked up the cups. "Come on in. I'll introduce you to the guys."

"I don't want to intrude on y'all's guy time." I hadn't really thought past the getting-here part.

"You aren't intruding. I love that you surprised me. And with a milkshake."

There was that word.

He squeezed my hand. "The guys want to meet you."

I looped my arm around his. "Lead the way. Sorry I didn't bring enough to share."

He kissed the top of my head. "I'm really glad you came."

Joji was right. Being lovable was more about the willingness to love.

* * *

THAT NIGHT after tucking into bed, I texted my mom. *I've been dating someone.*

As I hit send, I tried to remember that her response wasn't as much about me as it was about her.

But that didn't stop my stomach from twisting into a knot.

CHAPTER 19

Clint had stopped showing up regularly, and my reputation as a successful matchmaker was in jeopardy. But I had a plan in the works.

"Harper, would you call this a squeak?" I opened and closed the barn door, changing the speed to try and get the door to make a sound.

He scratched his head. "Maybe. Have any of that spray? I can squirt the hinges."

"No. I'll tell Clint. He needs reasons to come over." I walked down the row of stalls, checking each door. "I'm just hoping that one day when he's with Joji, he'll realize how much he loves her. Everyone can tell."

"How can you tell?" Harper tested the doors on the other side of the barn.

"The way he looks at her. And he shows up over here every time I call him about something that needs fixing. It's not even his farm." I sighed. "Any advice on making him realize how he feels?"

"Nope. The man has to decide for himself."

"Not even Job has that kind of patience." I walked outside and looked under the eaves. "Oh! Maybe we could find a wasp nest. Then he'd have to come spray it."

Harper grabbed my hand. "Leave the poor man alone. He can figure out his own love life."

"Are you sure? I'm really worried that he's going to miss out on happiness with Joji." I made sure all the goats were in their proper places, then closed up the barn. "This coming week, Joji is going to teach me to make cheese. That'll be exciting."

"I'll ask my sister for recipes." He led me toward the trailer. "Let's go inside. I want to chat with you about something."

"Do you really mean chat or is this one of those we-need-to-talk conversations? Because I have an allergy to those."

He stopped and kissed my hand. "We can chat here. Would you be interested in driving up to Dallas with me? I'd like for you to meet my family."

Blood pooled in my feet, and I grabbed his shirt to keep from falling over. I knew how much his family meant to him. "I'd love that. When would we go?"

"A month from this weekend. I'm not working then. And if Joji doesn't mind you being gone, we could leave on Friday and come home on Monday."

"I'll ask her." I smiled, wishing my insides would stop shaking. Pulling away, I headed into the trailer.

"Cami, if it's too soon, we can wait." He caught up to me.

I shook my head but didn't turn around. I didn't want him to see my tears. "I want to meet your family."

"But?" He stepped around me and waited for me to look up.

"Does your family know we're dating?"

"They've known for a while. And Mom has been asking about when she gets to meet you."

"I told my mom about you. She finally called me back."

His lips pulled into a tight line.

I tried to keep my emotions in check. "She gave me her patronizing 'that's nice' as if I'd mentioned getting a new shirt."

"Cami, it's you I care about."

"I know that if they met you, they'd adore you, and I think they'd be proud of me. Finally, they'd like one of my choices." I hadn't given up hope that my parents still wanted me as a daughter.

"Whenever they want to meet me, I'll be there." He took both of my hands in his. "But please, don't let worry consume you. It won't hurt my feelings if they never want to meet me."

"If that was supposed to make me feel better, it didn't." I sucked in a stuttered breath, shoving back the sobs that threatened. "They are my parents. And I won't be okay if this is how it's going to be forever. I've been cut off, and I hate feeling like I'm the biggest disappointment in their life."

His jaw clenched. "I want *you* to be happy."

"Thank you." I buried my face in his chest. "Maybe at Thanksgiving. Are you working that day?"

"Not sure yet, but I'll keep an eye on the calendar. We'll figure it out." He kissed the top of my head. "I can't wait for you to meet my family. Everyone is going to love you."

Harper always tried to focus on the happier side of life. I wished I knew how to forget the needling hurts that bothered me. But I hadn't figured out how to ignore them completely.

* * *

BLEARY EYED, I walked out to the barn. I'd been up till all hours telling Harper about how Clint had finally come to his senses. And truth be told, I couldn't take credit for his lightbulb moment. Not that I hadn't messaged him about burned-out bulbs all over the farm.

Harper had been right. Clint figured it out on his own.

I prepped the new machine for milking. I'd only used it twice before, and I still needed to think about every step. Once I had everything out, I escorted the goats into the barn. They ran into position because they were excited about the food waiting for them. They'd adjusted to the new contraption faster than I had.

After locking each of them into place, I made my way down the line, attaching each goat to the machine. When I made it to the last goat, I blinked and rubbed my eyes.

"Cami, what are you doing?" Clint always showed up in the barn when I preferred he stay far away.

"Milking goats. Duh."

"Where do you plan to attach that piece on that goat you're looking at?"

I looked from Clint to the goat, and my horror erupted as laughter. "I almost made his day, didn't I?" I led the stud back to his pen before trying to explain. "The goats and I have an understanding. I don't get all up in their business, and things stay peaceful. He must've gotten into the ladies' pen last night. Because he came trotting out with them, and that was the only pen I opened."

"Knowing the difference between nannies and billies is important." He turned on the machine. "Thanks for helping Joji. She likes having you here."

"I like being here. Goats and all. And I'll figure things out so that I never make that mistake again."

"Good. I'll take over here if you want to feed the chickens."

"Already fed them."

"Any chance you'd make me a cup of coffee?" Clint lifted his eyebrows, silently pleading.

"Sure thing, cowboy." I ran back to the trailer, eager to help Clint, and happy to feel appreciated.

Even when he laughed at my silly mistakes, Clint didn't make me feel like a disappointment.

CHAPTER 20

The wind caught my dress as I stepped out of the trailer. Grabbing at the fabric, I laughed. "I feel ridiculous."

"But you look very historical. Mostly. Your hair is a bit modern, but the designer can work her magic on that." Haley opened the passenger-side door of her car.

I wadded up my dress and climbed inside. "Where are we doing this photo shoot?"

"The ranch. I mentioned to Joji that my client wanted a picture of you with a horse. She talked to Clint, and voila. He set up everything."

"Great. A horse. I'm barely comfortable around goats and chickens."

"Whatever. I've seen the way you talk to them." Haley laughed.

"Some of them are good listeners."

Boingo wasn't, but I didn't want to bring up that conversation.

She parked next to a field, and a guy waved. Next to him was a horse. A big one.

"That's Parker. He's the wrangler." Haley gathered her camera equipment.

I tried not to trip on my petticoat as I climbed out of the car. "What's a wrangler?"

"He takes care of the horses."

"Is he the one who will save me if the horse goes darting off like it's seen a ghost?"

Haley rolled her eyes. "I wasn't planning on you actually being on the horse. Just next to it."

"Okay. So he'll step in if I'm being trampled." I knew how to get laughs out of Haley, and today, I worked that skill.

"Afternoon, ladies. This here is Calliope. I did a little research, so hopefully, the way she's done up looks enough like Little House on the Prairie. You sure look the part." Parker tipped his hat.

I curtsied. And that set Haley to laughing again.

"All right. Let's get this started." She scanned the area, and it was obvious her creative juices were bubbling.

I slipped my phone out of the pocket of the dress. I loved that this costume had pockets. Then I snapped a picture of her. With her red curls blowing in the wind, she looked like the model.

"Mind if I post this?" I showed her the photo.

Her cheeks colored a bit. "Sure."

I posted the picture then moved closer to Calliope.

Parker handed me the reins. "She's a sweetie. Won't hurt a fly." He dropped sugar cubes into my hand. "And you can give her these."

I patted Calliope on the nose. "How do you feel about being on a book cover?"

She tossed her head as if she approved.

"Good. Make sure you get a few extra carrots out of the deal." I let her have her sweet treat. "That's why I do it. Not for carrots. I prefer green stuff."

While I talked to the horse, Haley moved around composing her images.

I trusted her to make me look good.

"Turn your head toward me." She continued moving.

As I turned to face her, my breath caught. Harper was sitting on the fence, watching me. My smile was involuntary.

"Perfect. Exactly like that." Haley clicked the shutter over and over. "I think that does it. These are going to be great." She nodded toward Harper. "You can go talk to him."

As soon as Parker had the reins, I ran toward Harper. "Hi."

He let his gaze slide down my dress as he hopped off the fence. "I'm going to have quite a collection of books that I'll never read."

"You haven't seriously ordered all the books I've modeled for, have you?"

He nodded. "I asked Haley for a list. And when the leopard-shifter book arrived, I thought Eli was going to hurt himself laughing."

"What a stinker. He might get a few other shifter books put in his stocking this Christmas. Just for fun. Or better yet, maybe I'll give him a gift certificate to Delaney's shop."

Harper howled with laughter. "I think I love that idea. I'll pitch in."

"How did you know where to find me?"

"Joji. I showed up at your place, hoping to take you to lunch."

"Lunch would be so fun, but I told Joji that I'd—"

He put up his hand. "She said to tell you she'd take care of it."

The twinkle in his green eyes made it clear he had a surprise, and he'd done some planning. How could he know it was my birthday? I hadn't said a word about it.

Whatever the reason, I was happy to enjoy time with him.

"We have to be quick because I have to be at the studio in just over an hour."

Haley laughed. "See you tomorrow."

Harper's smile widened. "Looks like you're off for the afternoon."

I glanced over at Haley. "Are you sure?"

She nodded. "Have fun."

"I definitely need to change first." I grabbed his hand.

"You look pretty cute." He lifted an eyebrow.

"I have to return it. And I don't trust myself not to spill food down the front." I giggled as he swept me into his arms.

"Then I'll take you home first."

As he carried me to his truck, I could hear the click of Haley's camera. I wanted the pictures, but I wouldn't need them to remember this moment.

As I buckled into my seat, my phone buzzed. And I laughed when I read the message.

"What's so funny?" Harper started the engine.

"I posted a picture of Haley a bit ago. Zach texted that he's going to need the original."

"Makes sense. The man's in love." Harper winked.

Was he talking about Zach? Because just then, it felt like the statement was much more personal.

Harper stopped outside the trailer.

"Come on in. I'll be quick." I pushed open the front door. Some days, I didn't bother locking up. But at night, I always bolted the door.

After shedding the dress and petticoat, I changed into comfy clothes. I walked into the living room wearing jeans and a long-sleeved top. "I'm ready. Where are we going to eat?"

"It's a surprise."

"Now you have me as curious as a cat." I hadn't

mentioned my birthday because I didn't want it to sound like I was asking for attention.

At the moment, my thinking didn't make as much sense, but saying it now seemed even worse. If I popped out with "Oh, by the way. Today is my birthday," that would put him on the spot and make him feel bad for not getting me a present.

I didn't want that. I just wanted... him.

He smiled as he opened the door. Could he read my thoughts? Did he feel the same way?

When he kissed me after helping me into the truck, I was nearly convinced he knew every thought in my head.

While my thoughts were swirling, he drove back roads that seemed vaguely familiar.

When he pulled up to the big gate at Lilith's venue, I recognized where we were. It was officially named Stargazer Springs Ranch Getaway, but that wasn't what we called it. After he punched in the code, the gate opened, and Harper drove out toward the river.

"I thought a picnic would be nice. And Lilith told me about a beautiful spot here by the river." He pointed at a blanket spread out on the ground. Pillows were piled on one side, and a cooler held down another corner. "I was hoping it hadn't blown away in this breeze."

I jumped out and ran to the spot. "I don't know what to say. This is amazing."

He wrapped his arms around me from behind. "When we met, you were almost twenty-five. Or was it nearly? That's not true anymore, is it?"

My brain kicked into high gear as I tried to guess how he'd discovered that it was my birthday. "Did Joji tell you? I haven't mentioned it to anyone, but I think I had to put my birthday on one of the forms I filled out to get paid."

"It wasn't Joji."

"I also filled out forms at the photography studio, but no one there even mentioned my birthday. Was it Haley? How did you know?"

"You showed me your license." He pressed his clean-shaven cheek to mine. "Remember?"

I nodded. "I can't believe you remembered."

"It's been on my calendar." He kissed my cheek. "Have a seat. I need to grab something from the truck."

I sat down on the blanket and tried organizing my thoughts. He deserved an explanation about why I hadn't said anything about my birthday.

He set a big gift down next to me. "Happy birthday, Cami."

"Before I open this, I need to tell you why I stayed quiet about it."

"Only if you want to. It doesn't matter."

"It does matter. I didn't want it to seem like I was asking for attention. You give it freely, but… I don't know. Jumping around and announcing that it was my birthday didn't seem like something a grownup would do."

"I think it depends on the person. Not on whether they are grown up. Open your gift."

I pulled tissue paper out of the top of the bag. "Harper! You bought me boots!" I yanked off my tennis shoes before pulling the turquoise boots out of the box.

He laughed at my excitement. "I hope they fit. I had to snoop a little and guess."

Once they were on, I stood up and spun in a circle. "I love them."

"I've seen you tromping around that farm in rain boots and figured you could use a pair of real boots."

"If you think I'm wearing these while working on the farm, you're so very wrong. That would only mess them up."

I dropped down next to him. "Thank you. They're perfect. This is perfect. And I'm sorry I didn't say something earlier."

He tucked a strand of hair behind my ear. "I love you, Cami."

And that was the best birthday present ever.

I caught his lips with mine. "Good. Because I am completely in love with you too."

* * *

AFTER AN EXTENDED LUNCH WITH HARPER, I said goodbye because I'd made plans with Tessa and Delaney. I wasn't going to shirk my friend duties. And I liked hanging out with them.

I knocked on Tessa's door, prepared to apologize for not telling them it was my birthday.

When it swung open, a loud "Surprise!" erupted.

I'd been more than a little bit wrong about nobody knowing it was my birthday.

After hugging all my friends, I kissed Harper. "You know how to keep a secret."

"Only when it involves a happy surprise." He tweaked my nose. "And it turns out, a lot of people knew it was your birthday. Tessa called me a few days ago to tell me about these plans."

I glanced at my phone when it buzzed. My mom texted: *Happy Birthday. I hope you had a good day.*

I tapped out a quick reply. *The best. Thanks.*

Then, I snapped a picture of the incredible cake Tessa had made and posted it for all the world to see. Or at least anyone who cared enough to look at my posts.

I captioned it. *Happy birthday to me.*

CHAPTER 21

The chill in the air had permeated the barn, and I pulled my sweater closed before walking down the line and attaching the goats to the milking machine. This contraption made milking them so much easier. And it made for cool photos.

With the milking goats all lined up, I angled my phone just right and snapped a picture.

Harper was picking me up in an hour, but I really wanted to see Joji's reaction to the new accessories I'd gotten for the goats. And Clint's too.

He'd been over here a lot more. I wouldn't have to be searching for reasons to message him day after day.

When laughter sounded outside the barn, I held my breath.

"Look at all those guys all dolled up with bowties." Joji clapped as she laughed.

Clint groaned as the door opened. "She said she'd find a way to tell the billies from the nannies, but I'm not sure about her solution."

Joji threw her hands in the air. "Look at those pretty girls! They have bows on their heads! How cute."

"You realize the goats are just going to eat all this stuff, right?" Clint shook his head.

My joy disintegrated. "You think so?"

Amusement creased at the corners of his eyes. "Goats eat everything."

"True, but the pictures will be cute on the website. I've been working on putting one together. Because if you make people love your goats, then they'll really love your cheese."

Joji rubbed Clint's arm and smiled up at him. "She's right. That would be great, Cami. When you get back, we'll talk about the website some more." Joji walked down the line, greeting each goat. "What time are you headed out?"

"Harper will be here in an hour."

"Go get ready. We've got this." She hugged me. "And have fun. Oh! Here's something to read. Remember my friend Tandy? It's one of her books." Joji fanned herself, then winked.

"Thanks." I hugged the book to my chest and ran back to the trailer. I didn't want to smell like a goat when I met Harper's family.

Before our scheduled departure time, I showered, dressed, and packed. Well, I'd been packed for a week. But I changed out outfits, second-guessing my choices. I'd done that often.

I wanted them to like me. Needed, really.

Today, my nerves were in knots. I was both terrified and excited to meet his family. But when I opened my door, all my terror faded away when I saw Harper's smile.

He loved me, and nothing would change that.

"Morning, gorgeous." He didn't make it more than one step in the door before I was in his arms.

I buried my face in the curve of his neck as his muscular arms tightened around me. "I love you too."

A chuckle rumbled in his chest.

"I shouldn't have added the too, but when I saw you, I was thinking about how you love me, so I added the too even though you hadn't said it first."

"I do love you, and I hope you hear it in every 'morning, gorgeous' and 'hello, dear' I ever say."

I sighed as he set me on my feet. "You think they'll like me? I mean, I know it doesn't matter, but it would be easier if they did."

He cupped my face. "They're going to love you."

"Okay, then I'm ready." I picked up my bag. "And I have coffee ready to go for both of us."

"Perfect." He carried my bag out and tossed it into the back seat.

Smelling like a rose, I buckled into my seat. "How long is the drive? Will we stop somewhere along the way?"

"You must be a blast on long road trips." He laughed. "It'll be about five hours. And we'll stop in San Saba or Goldthwaite." He lifted a gift bag out of the backseat. "For you."

I yanked the pretty tissue paper out of the top before pulling out a cute embroidered pillow. It looked nothing like the one Chase had given me, and it was beautiful. "I love it."

"I figured if you wanted to sleep during the trip, you could use that." He turned onto the road and headed toward the highway.

Holding up my book, I laughed. "Joji gave me this, so I'm not sure I'll be sleeping."

He rubbed the back of his neck. "Seriously?"

"What? Are you jealous?" I glanced at the cover. "You shouldn't be. This guy hasn't got anything on..." My gaze landed on the cover model's shoulder. A scar, less noticeable than the one in real life, was there in the very same spot I'd kissed. I grabbed Harper's hand. "This is you."

"Why would you say that? You can't even see the face because of the cowboy hat."

"Now I *really* want to see you in a cowboy hat. But this is you." I squeezed his hand. "This is so cool. Why didn't you tell me you modeled for a book cover?"

"I only did it once with the stipulation that my face wouldn't be visible. I didn't count on anyone identifying me by my chest."

"It's a nice chest." I stared at the cover another minute. "But I won't tell."

"Thank you. The writer asked me—begged me—to pose, and right after buying the house, the little bit of extra cash was nice." His shoulders relaxed. "In fact, one of the ladies that I've seen at those goat yoga sessions is the photographer who took that picture."

"Lilith? That's the ranch owner's wife. His name is Beau, I think."

Harper laughed. "I met him too. But that was before he and Lilith figured things out."

"People are falling in love left and right on that ranch. It's kind of fun." I tucked the book in my purse. "I'll keep it hidden when we're with your family. Just in case someone else might recognize your chest."

"That would be embarrassing. My sisters would *never* let me live that down."

"If it comes up, we'll distract them with my leopard-costume story."

"Good plan. It's one of my favorite stories."

I kissed his hand. "Just so you know, I think the whole book-cover thing is really cool. And now I know why your ears turn red whenever I talk about posing for covers."

"You have me all figured out, don't you?" He winked, but

ONE CHOICE I'D NEVER MAKE

the look in his eyes conveyed a more serious emotion. "We've talked a bit about your exes."

"They all live in Texas." I hoped and prayed that he'd at least chuckle at my joke.

Thankfully, he did. "I'm not suggesting we talk about them again. And I see no need to bring up mine except to say..." He pulled his hand away and scrubbed his face. "My family is outrageously excited—I think those were my mom's exact words—because this is the first time I've brought someone home for them to meet." His gaze fixed on the traffic in front of him, he laid his open hand on the center console.

Of course I grabbed it. "You have this amazing way of making me feel like a prize. And I think I might cry. Happy tears."

"You are a prize. Anyone who makes you feel otherwise is... wrong." His hand tightened around mine. "You're the whole enchilada. Smart. Funny. Adventurous. And beautiful to boot."

"Maybe when we stop, we can get some Mexican food. I think I want enchiladas." I fished a tissue out of my purse, using only one hand. It would take more than crying to make me let go of Harper right now.

In fact, I never wanted to let go.

HARPER SQUEEZED MY HAND.

I opened my eyes as I lifted my head off the pillow. "I'm sorry I fell asleep."

"It's fine, but we're almost there." Excitement danced in his eyes.

I'd waited a long time to be the reason someone looked so excited.

He parked along the curb in front of a large one-story. "That's the tree. I'd climb it, then try to get up on the roof."

"Why the roof?"

"To jump off. My friend and I used to drag my mattress into the backyard. It made landing a lot easier."

"How are you still alive?"

"My mom would usually figure out what we were doing after about the second jump. Then game over." He smiled and motioned toward the front door. "The welcoming committee has gathered. Are you ready for this?"

"So ready."

He jumped out and opened my door. "And here's a kiss for luck. You won't need it, but it will please the crowd."

After a short toe-curling kiss, I scanned the smiling faces and waved. "How old is your baby sister?" Our age difference hadn't seemed like a big deal, but looking at his family, I suddenly felt very young.

"A little older than you, but it doesn't matter. Not to them. Not to me."

I appreciated his hand on my back as we made our way up the sidewalk.

Mrs. Harper was the first one down the steps. "You have no idea how excited we are to meet you." With her arms around me, she moved me side to side. It was somewhere between a dance move and a hug. "And you are just gorgeous. Let me introduce you to everyone. I'm Melanie, but everyone calls me Mel. Unless you prefer Mom." She turned and faced her family. "This is my husband Evan. And my daughters Erin, Emmy, and Elisa. Diego is in the kitchen making brownies for later. And the other guys will be here in a bit with the little ones. They ran them over to the park to get some wiggles out."

Names swirled in my head. This family really liked the

letter e. "I'm Cami. And I'm so happy to be here. Harper has told me so much about y'all."

Mel hugged her son. "Ethan sure surprised us. When he called and said there was someone he wanted us to meet, I thought maybe he'd gotten a dog. This is so much better."

Elisa, or maybe it was Emmy, pushed open the door. "Let's go inside. No point standing around out here."

Harper's hand tightened around mine as we walked inside.

I hoped this was the first of many times that I'd get to visit this house. Two steps inside, and I already felt at home.

CHAPTER 22

After a family dinner that was like a scene out of a Hallmark movie, we all settled in the living room with our brownie sundaes. And these were by far the best brownies I'd ever tasted. Before we left, I was asking for recipes.

I snuggled up on one end of the couch with Harper next to me. His parents were cuddled on a love seat. The other couples were seated together in different parts of the room, some on chairs, others on the floor. And in the middle of the room, the kiddos sat on a blanket enjoying dessert.

As people talked and laughed and shared stories, I worked on putting names with faces. I wanted to remember everything about tonight. I wasn't used to big family gatherings. Who knew that I'd love this so much?

Figuring out which e-name went with which sister was easier now that they had husbands beside them, and conveniently they'd married alphabetically. Erin, the oldest, had married Anthony. Elisa married Ben. And the baby of the family, Emmy, was still in the newlywed phase with Diego.

The gap in the middle wasn't lost on me. It was as if I'd

been scripted into this story long before I'd shimmied into that leopard suit.

As soon as I finished my ice cream, Harper jumped up. "I'll take that into the kitchen for you. Need anything else?"

"I'm good." I smiled up at him. "Really good."

He beamed. "Be right back."

"Honey, just put those in the dishwasher. I'll start it before I go to bed," Mel said.

"Will do."

When Harper returned, he sat on the floor in front of the couch. The family's chocolate lab lay down next to him, and within seconds, his nieces and nephew crawled into his lap.

I watched them play as the family continued sharing stories and asking me questions. And it didn't feel awkward. It wasn't an interrogation so much as genuine interest.

Resting a hand on Harper's shoulder, I leaned forward almost giddy about telling his family the leopard costume story. "I'm not sure if he's told you how we met."

He reached back and grabbed my hand.

Emmy shook her head. "He hasn't, and it wasn't for lack of asking."

"He kept quiet because of me. Most people would call it embarrassing, but whatever. It's quite a tale."

Harper laughed out loud, startling his little niece. Humor-wise, he and I were well-matched.

I cleared my throat, getting ready to entertain. "On the side, I sometimes pose as a model. Mostly for authors who want pictures for book covers."

Mel patted Evan's leg. "Not a surprise. She's gorgeous. Just like I told ya."

"Well, for one photo shoot, I didn't remember to bring a change of clothes with me. So after we finished, there I was in downtown San Antonio in a skin-tight leopard costume walking the streets as the sun went down."

Gasps and chuckles sounded throughout the room.

"It didn't seem like a big deal until I realized someone was following me."

Emmy pointed at her brother. "Seriously, Ethan? You probably scared her to death."

"I wasn't following her." He looked up at me. "Mostly because I hadn't seen her yet."

"I don't even know the name of the guy who was chasing after me. But anyway, to get to where I was parked, I had to walk through an alley. That alley was all that separated me from the safety of my car. In high-heeled boots, running was risky. I did it anyway. Then just like a scene out of a movie, this guy walks into view at the other end of the alley." I kissed the top of Harper's head. "So I threw my arms around him and told him I was being followed."

"The poor guy trying to return her dropped tail seemed very confused." Harper grinned. "And so was I when Cami ran off without the tail."

Enthralled by the story, Mel leaned forward. "How did you find her?"

"We have mutual friends. I showed up to a pool party a few days after she dropped her tail, and there she was, sitting on the edge of the pool."

"I didn't run away that time. In fact, I threw my arms around him again. He's rather huggable."

"That might be the sweetest thing I've ever heard." Erin stood. "Cami, I think it's only fair that we tell you stories about my brother."

He groaned.

"But first, I need to get my kiddos in bed. Don't start without me." She carried her kids down the hall.

Elisa followed.

Harper shifted back to the couch. "I'm tired. You ready for bed?"

"Not a chance, buddy. This is the good stuff." I tucked closer to him as he put an arm around me.

"Just promise that you'll still like me when the stories are over."

I kept my voice low so that only he could hear my answer. "Change that like to love, and I promise."

He planted a quick kiss on the side of my head. "Deal."

When Erin and Elisa walked back into the room, Emmy waved her hand. "I'll go first. This is a good story. It's only right that we start with something that makes him look good."

The family laughed as if they all knew what was coming.

"There was this pizza place that I'd go to with friends or on dates. And it wasn't unusual for Ethan and his friend to show up there on nights that I had a date. He's such a big brother. Anyway, he wouldn't say anything to me or even come to the table, but he'd show up just to see how my date was behaving."

"I trained him well." Evan grinned. It was clear the man was proud of his son.

"Well, this one night, I was on a first date and we were having pizza before going to the movies. I managed to spill a drink all down the front of my T-shirt—a white one. Embarrassed, I ran to the restroom. A minute later, Ethan knocks before walking into the ladies' room. My brother pulled off his shirt and said that we should trade. He looked completely ridiculous in a T-shirt that was too small for him. It was hilarious. And he stretched out that shirt, but he saved my date." She pointed at Elisa. "Your turn."

Elisa flashed a mischievous grin. "Ethan thinks he's funny."

I laughed. "This one isn't going to make you look as good, is it?"

He shook his head. "Nope. Remember your promise."

"Since we have the pool out back, my friends would come over a lot during the summer and spend the night. It wasn't unusual to have several swimsuits hanging in the bathroom," Elisa said.

"It was a mess." He didn't seem to mind being in the hot seat and having his family tell stories about him.

Elisa rolled her eyes. "One morning, we got up, and there were no swimsuits in the bathroom. He'd wet them and shoved them in the freezer. It took us forever to thaw them with the blow dryer."

"They should've just tossed them in the pool." Harper grinned like a little boy.

As the stories continued, I snuggled closer. My sweetheart was a guy who loved pranks, always tried to make people laugh, and would literally give someone the shirt off his back.

As the stories were winding down, Anthony spoke up for the first time. "I have one. Emmy said he was such a big brother, and that's true. Even as a little brother, he tried to be the big brother. Erin and I started dating when we were in middle school. And we had a few spats over the years."

"Only two." Erin kissed his cheek.

"Once when Erin and I were having a disagreement, I pulled up in front, and she jumped out of the car, sobbing. I didn't even make it halfway up the walk before Ethan was in my face. Well, he would've been in my face had he been taller. I think you were eight, maybe nine. And he hauled off and slugged me, yelling at me the whole time for making his sister cry. Erin came to my rescue, so I sort of won big that day." He rubbed his cheek. "But it hurt."

"Sorry about that." Harper rubbed the back of his neck.

I covered a yawn as I laughed. It was way past my normal bedtime. "That story makes so much sense."

He looked down at me with an apologetic smile. "There is a possibility I might've hit him."

I knew exactly who he meant. "I know."

Mel clapped. "Enough stories. We need to let our guest get some sleep." She jumped up. "Follow me."

Harper picked up our bags, which hadn't moved since we'd dropped them just inside the door.

"Y'all are in here." She pushed open a door.

Harper stopped. "What about putting her in Emmy's room?"

"Elisa is in there. And Erin is in her room. Emmy is the only one not staying here tonight. She and Diego are headed home. They are still in the honeymoon phase… if you know what I mean."

"Mom, pretty sure we know exactly what you mean. Good night."

She walked out, then opened the door again. "Oh, and Shap is in here with you tonight."

Harper looked from the chocolate lab back to his mom. "Seriously?"

"Sleep tight." Laughing, she closed the door.

"Just then, your mom called him Shap, but I thought his name was Chap. Like Cheerio, old chap. He's cute. He reminds me of Bones."

"Spelled like Chap, said like Shap." Harper stared at the dog. "Before I tell you what his name is short for, I have to tell you about Champ." Harper moved my bag to the bed. "Change first. Bathroom is across the hall if you need it. I'll make myself scarce for a few minutes."

"I'll change in the bathroom. You don't have to leave." I picked up my bag. "I'll hurry because I want to hear the story."

I changed quickly, glad that I'd packed something decent.

When I walked back into the room, he was in lounge

pants and a T-shirt. He started the story as soon as I closed the door. "So, right after Erin started dating Anthony, Dad brought home a dog. We called him Champ. He was a black lab, and Dad trained that dog. But sadly, Champ got out one day, and a car hit him. We were all devastated. Only a few days later, Dad brought home another dog, Chap. And Dad trained this dog just like he'd trained Champ. Chap is short for Chaperone. Let me demonstrate." Harper sat down next to me on the bed.

Chap sat down in front of Harper and stared.

Then Harper clasped my hand.

Chap barked, only once and quietly.

"That's only the beginning. If I turn off the lamp, he'll bark until I turn it back on."

"That's hysterical."

"It wasn't for my sisters. And there's more." Harper draped an arm around me and kissed me.

Chap barked twice.

"Thanks to Chap, my dad always knew what was going on in the living room. You can see why I never subjected anyone else to this. And I really didn't plan on having to deal with it this weekend. Lay down, I'll show you his other trick."

I stretched out on the bed. "Okay?"

Chap jumped up and lay down beside me. And when Harper moved closer to me, Chap gave a low growl.

"He stands guard and is trained to call for help when needed." Harper lay down on top of me, which was not at all unpleasant.

I slipped my arms around him. "I don't see a problem."

Chap stopped growling and was quiet only a second, his gaze fixed on Harper.

When Harper's lips met mine, Chap went nuts.

Laughing, I covered my ears. "How do you make him stop?"

Harper gave me another quick kiss before stepping away. "An arm's length distance is usually enough to calm him down."

Laughter echoed in the hall. If it weren't so funny, I would've been embarrassed. The whole house knew what was happening in the bedroom.

Harper lowered his voice. "But I came prepared. See, one night I spotted Elisa and Ben on the porch swing in the back. They were kissing away, and Chap hadn't made a sound. It wasn't because they'd locked him inside. Ben had brought chew treats with him. To this day, I don't think my dad has any idea. Anyway, I brought some with me." He dug a treat out of his bag and tossed it on the floor.

Tail wagging, Chap settled down and started chewing.

Harper stretched out next to me. "Dog or no dog, I'll be a gentleman, but I don't want to listen to him bark."

I snuggled up next to him and laughed when Chap climbed onto the foot of the bed with that treat in his mouth. "I'm not sure he completely trusts you."

"Are you glad you came?"

"Harper, I love your family. Today has been wonderful. And I feel like I know you better."

Staring at the ceiling, he ran his fingers through my hair. "They love you too. I knew they would." He dropped a kiss onto the top of my head. "I love you, Cami."

I lifted my head to meet his gaze. "I love you too. So much."

He kissed me again, and Chap was too busy chewing on his treat to care.

* * *

When I woke up, the dog was snoring away, stretched out between Harper and me.

"Morning. How about a cup of coffee on the porch swing?" Harper reached over the dog and stroked my cheek.

"Sounds perfect."

"I'll meet you out there. Come on, Chap."

The dog stretched, then followed Harper out of the room.

Before changing out of my pajamas, I texted Tessa and Delaney. *Weekend is going great. He still loves me.*

Delaney responded first. *Duh. As if anything would change that.* She followed her text with a wink.

Tessa replied a second later. *So happy for you.*

After slipping on jeans and a shirt, I walked into the kitchen and stopped when I noticed Harper outside talking to his dad. I couldn't read lips, so I had no idea what they were saying, but the I'm-proud-of-you-son pat on the back was unmistakable.

I wanted that conversation to be about me. And maybe it was.

The whole scene made me happy. And it made me hurt.

After this weekend, I wanted my parents to meet Harper even more than before, but nothing about my family was like his.

CHAPTER 23

Joji sat down on the milking stool. "Tell me about the weekend. I want to hear everything. All. Of. It." She pointed at me. "Then we're going to talk more about your knack for social media. I've been stalking the pages you're running. If that's even what it's called."

"Managing, and I can't wait to talk about that. But first, the good stuff. I know why Harper is so funny and warm. His family is like that. I had such a good time. And I thought a lot about what you told me about love."

"And? I know there are parts you're leaving out."

I snapped a picture of the goats eating away while the machine did its thing. "You already know that Harper loves me. Still the best birthday present ever. His family made me feel right at home. He said they loved me." I danced in a circle. "So, that was something."

She hugged me. "Of course they love you. He's a lucky guy. What else?"

"They have a dog that looks so much like Bones." I told her all about Chap and how he was trained.

When she finally stopped laughing, the machine was finished with the milking.

"Let's get these ladies back in their pen, then I'll make you breakfast. We can talk about the website and social media. Haley said their bookings went way up when you started posting for them."

"I guess. It's fun for me." I latched the gate after escorting the nannies back to where they belonged. "When I look around here, I see all these little things that make me fall in love with the place. I mean, who wouldn't smile at a photo of a llama?"

"It's fun having them here, isn't it? They are my second favorite birthday gift." Joji waved to the temperamental pack animals.

"Imagine how people would react to pictures of Boingo in a tree." As we walked to the house, I continued pointing out sights that would endear people to the farm and her cheese. "That's my two cents."

"What do I need to do to set up one of these accounts?"

"It's easy. I can show you."

"And you'll manage it for me?" Joji tied on an apron and started slicing bread.

"Absolutely." I enjoyed working on the farm, but I loved all the stuff I did on social media and seeing how it helped the studio and Tessa. "And we definitely need pictures of your cheese toast."

She grinned. "And of my garden when I finally plant something. Maybe even a picture of Clint if he'll allow it."

"It's all in how you ask."

She laughed. "Smart girl."

I spent the rest of the morning eating cheese toast and helping her get an account set up. Then I raced over to the studio.

Haley was waiting at my desk. "Soooo? How'd the weekend go? Is he still your superhero?"

"More than ever." I pressed a hand to my heart. "His family loves me."

Haley threw her arms around me, and Nacha cheered.

"When did you sneak in?" I turned and hugged her.

"I was in my office and heard the good news. I'm happy for you."

I sighed. "Now if I can just get my parents to agree to meet him. They don't call me back that often because I'm off doing my own thing. That's how Mom puts it. Dad just doesn't talk to me."

Nacha hugged me again. "Cami, I know that's hard. But always remember that you have family here. Blood isn't what makes us family."

I nodded, but it didn't make the sting go away. It hurt that people who were strangers a year ago cared more about me than my parents.

If I could just get them to meet Harper, they'd see that I had a handle on life and that I'd figured out how to be an adult.

They'd be proud of me.

* * *

FOR THE NEXT TWO WEEKS, wonderful things happened, and life continued to improve. Things were still dicey with my parents, but even in that department, there was good news.

Side by side, Harper and I stood in my kitchen, making dinner. Emmy and Diego had sent a few recipes, and so far, everything Harper and I had tried making tasted amazing.

"So I told you how Joji had me start managing her social media for the farm. And then Lilith asked me if I'd be interested in managing the social for the venue. Those pictures of the picnic were perfect for that! Well, guess who called me today and wants me to run her social media?"

His brow pinched. "You already run Tessa's page for the doughnut shop. And the one for the studio. Are you going to do one for the lingerie shop? Will there be modeling involved?" He danced his eyebrows.

"Modeling yes, but not by me. And not lingerie. Tandy called me."

The adorable red colored his ears.

"And since I choose what to post, guess which cover will not go up on her social media page?"

"Thank you."

I kissed his cheek. "You're welcome. I know all this extra stuff is keeping me busier, and I'm sorry."

"You clearly love it. And I'm happy to see you doing what you love." He slid the food onto plates as I held them out. "Let's hope this tastes as good as it looks."

"It looks fantastic."

During dinner, we chatted about how work was going for him and about the goats. Because we always talked about the goats. Then afterward, we cleaned up.

I wiped my hands, then hung the dishtowel over the stove handle. "Mom called me back today."

"Good."

His muted reaction irritated me.

"Isn't that exciting? I asked about going to visit for Thanksgiving, but Mom suggested that they drive here and meet us for dinner this weekend. It's not ideal, but they want to meet you. And I haven't seen them since I dropped my stuff off." I wanted him to share my hope that things were finally changing.

"I'm glad she called you."

"You don't sound glad. You sound miffed." I tried unsuccessfully to keep the edge out of my voice.

He scrubbed his face. "I'm concerned that you'll be disappointed again. It hurts to watch you get your hopes up only to have them shattered."

"You think I should just stop trying? Ignore them?"

"I'm not saying that. I don't know. Maybe I am. I don't like the way they treat you." He walked toward me.

I backed up. "They're my parents! You have your big happy family where everyone loves you and is proud of you. Don't you think I want that too?"

"Cami."

When he moved one step closer, I shook my head. "Just go." I walked into the kitchen so that I wouldn't have to see him leave.

The door closed quietly. I guess I was the only one with an urge to slam things.

Pacing in the living room, I was too angry to cry. And every time I walked toward the far wall, the happy couple who used to live on the farm mocked me from their happy little picture.

Slamming it to the ground would bring me all kinds of bad luck, but I could at least take it off the wall. When I did, a notecard fell to the ground.

I love you.

Words that I knew in my head penetrated my heart in a way they never had before.

I raced out the door, hoping to catch Harper before he pulled away.

And I nearly tripped over the man.

Harper was sitting on the top step, and Boingo was next to him with keys dangling out of his mouth.

After taking the keys away from Boingo, I nudged my way in between them and sat down. "I'm sorry." I handed Harper the notecard. "When did you hide that one?"

"I hid all of them on the same day. While Joji showed you

around the farm on that first day, I stashed notes in different places for you to find. I hid the one in the coffee cup after we unpacked that same night."

"That was months ago."

He nodded. "I knew then, but you were in a big transition period, and you didn't need me complicating it. I felt fairly sure you wouldn't find that one for a while."

I leaned my head on his shoulder, trying to ignore the idea that he now knew all the places I hadn't cleaned since moving in.

"And, Cami, *I'm* proud of you. My mom calls me all the time, excited about what you posted. Did you know that she follows every page you manage? She even started buying Tandy's books. Let's just hope she never figures out who is on that cover." He put his arm around me. "If your parents are disappointed, that's their issue. Not yours."

I wiped tears off my face.

"I will happily go with you to dinner to meet them. I will be pleasant and gracious. And *no matter what*, I'll be on my best behavior."

"Are you saying you won't slug my dad?"

"Yes." He pulled me closer. "But showing up and being nice, I'm not doing that for your parents. Not to impress them or to make them like me. I'm doing it because of you. Because I love you."

"Thank you. I want to give them one more chance. Mainly, so they can meet you."

"Let me know where and when. If I'm on the schedule, I'll find someone to cover my shift."

"If I'd known you were so incredible, I never would have left you standing on the sidewalk."

"Some women leave a glass slipper. Others leave a tail."

"I love you, Harper. No matter what happens with my parents." I needed him to know that deep in his bones.

"I know you do." He sounded sure.

"How did Boingo get your keys?"

"I gave them to him." He crinkled his nose and made a funny face. "It made sense at the time."

I climbed into his lap. Against the evening chill, he was warm.

Leaning a head on his shoulder, I burrowed even closer. "Because then you couldn't leave."

He rubbed my back. "There was no way I was going to leave."

"I should never have said that. I want the problem to go away. You aren't the problem."

He rested his head on mine. "Please don't let them make you think that you're the problem, Cami. You aren't."

"I think I know that. But I'm still not sure what to do." I shifted so that I could look him in the face. "Right now, all I want to do is just be here with you."

"And Boingo."

Boingo bleated after hearing his name.

I relished the security of Harper's arms, not for their strength, but because of the protective, unconditional love they represented. "He loves me."

Harper gave Boingo the side-eye.

I laughed. "But you love me more."

His breath tickled as he whispered in my ear. "Don't ever doubt that."

CHAPTER 24

I stopped in the middle of the living room and slid my hands down my skirt, smoothing out wrinkles. I'd splurged on a dress that would meet with my parents' approval. I felt a little bad about it until Harper arrived. After seeing the way his gaze traced my dress, I was thrilled with my purchase.

"Want me to smooth out those invisible wrinkles for you?" Harper danced his eyebrows.

"Very funny." I inhaled, then let out the breath slowly. My normal breathing techniques weren't helping me calm down. "Mom and Dad booked a reservation at the restaurant right down the road. That Cowboy Chef guy owns it. He's a big fan of Joji's cheese and has been out to the farm a few times." I paced in the trailer, checking the time every thirty seconds. "Have you met him?"

Harper wrapped his arms around me from behind. "Relax. Whatever happens tonight won't change the life you have here. Remember that."

I nodded. "Right. I'm trying not to get my hopes up." After

turning to face him, I straightened his tie. "You look amazing all dressed up."

"Cami, you can hope. Just remember that you aren't responsible for making them happy. You aren't responsible for making anyone happy."

"I know." I ran my hand down the lapel of his coat. "I know."

"We should go. Are you going to grab a coat?"

"No. I don't want to have to keep up with it. I'll only be running into the restaurant and back out to the truck."

My hands shook as I climbed into the passenger seat. My stomach was in knots, and I'd hardly eaten all day. But I didn't have long to worry. It only took three minutes to drive to the restaurant, and the whole time I fretted.

Since Mom and Dad had never been to my place, I wasn't even sure they knew how close it was. Not that it mattered.

Mom had probably read about the Cowboy Chef in some write-up.

Harper held my hand as we walked inside. My parents were already seated at a corner table.

Again, Dad had staked his turf first. Thinking about dinner as a warzone wasn't a great start. Another deep breath helped me maintain my smile.

The expression on Mom's face was rewarding. Harper was an amazing person, but he was also easy on the eyes. And Mom noticed.

"Mom, Dad, this is Harper." Excitement added a quiver to my voice. "Harper, these are my parents, David and Nora Phillips."

My dad extended his hand. "Pleased to meet you. I'd say we've heard so much about you, but she hasn't said much at all."

As tempting as it was to tell him that if he'd bothered to

talk to me I would have been happy to tell him all about Harper, I chose to keep the conversation steered in a more positive direction.

Mom made eye contact with me but only for a split second. I kept a smile plastered on my face as Harper and I took our seats. We hadn't even ordered, and I was beginning to regret coming to dinner.

I refocused on the goal. Having my parents meet Harper was why I was here. My family wasn't going to instantly morph into a TV sitcom family. But they were my parents, and Harper was the man I loved.

And the man I wanted to spend forever with. That hadn't come up in conversation, but we hadn't even dated a year.

Harper clasped my hand under the table, and that small gesture helped settle my thoughts.

I tried to think of something to say that would end the uncomfortable silence but wouldn't create an awkward conversation. "How are things at home?" A nice open-ended question was good, right?

Dad shifted in his chair. "We've already ordered drinks for everyone."

How did he know what we wanted?

Harper smiled. "Thanks."

"Before we order dinner, I just want to say that after giving it more thought, I might've been too harsh with you, Camille." My dad crossed his arms. "It's been months, and not once have you called asking for money or even hinting that you need help. You seem to have gained some independence during this rebellious streak of yours."

Until the rebellious part, I thought maybe I'd get the compliment I'd craved for so long.

Harper's hand tightened around mine.

My dad continued as if he were spreading good cheer. "If

you are happy with what you're doing, that's good. I hope one day you'll settle down a bit more, but I'm glad to see you've developed a strong work ethic."

"Thanks, Dad." I was surprised he came so close to an apology.

His words didn't hold the elation I thought would come when they accepted my choices, but from Dad, this was high praise. My dream that they wanted me to be happy was coming true. Why wasn't I giddy about it?

We ordered, and Mom filled me in on what all my former classmates were doing, which was basically a rehash of tidbits she'd already messaged.

"Listen to me going on and on. Harper, tell us about you. How did you meet Camille?"

"We met through mutual friends. At a pool party." He straightened his silverware. "She's a captivating woman, and I'm lucky I met her."

Mom pressed a hand to her heart. "How sweet. What do you do?"

My dad sat in silent judgment, but at least he wasn't frowning. I took that as a positive sign.

"I'm a fireman." Harper kept hold of my hand, letting his thumb brush against my skin.

My sweet boyfriend was the whole package, and I beamed as he answered. Then I noticed Dad's face turn to stone. It was worse than a frown. Hard and cold, his expression knotted my insides.

Harper hadn't said anything rude or out of line. Why was Dad reacting like that?

Mom's smile widened in the way it did when she was trying to make lemonade out of lemons. Not that she'd ever in her life actually made lemonade. She hired people to do that. "Oh? A fireman."

The waiter appeared with our food, and the awkward conversation hung in the air.

When our server walked away, Dad stared at Harper across the table. "I've given Camille room to explore what makes her happy, but I won't let her *ruin* her life. She'll marry a professional—someone more suited to her upbringing—because financial security is important. And *shift work* isn't going to get her that."

Harper tensed. "Sir, I love your daughter."

I squeezed his hand, hating that my dad would try to make Harper feel unworthy of me. I used to think the opposite was true, but now I knew better.

"Dad, please don't say that." I shot a look at Mom, wanting support, but she only stared at her food.

My father waved away my words. "I'm talking to Harper. If you *care* about my daughter... if you *care* about our relationship with her, then you'll get up from this table and walk away. I came here tonight hoping to smooth over the rockiness of the last few months. That can't happen with *you* in her life."

Flames seared my brain, and I squeezed hard on Harper's hand as he slid his chair back from the table. He wouldn't look at me, but I could see how angry he was. I also knew my hero would do anything if he thought it would make me happy.

If he thought I'd choose to live under my father's thumb rather than loving my hero, he was wrong. Nothing about that idea made me happy.

Harper had to know that. Right?

After giving my fingers a quick squeeze, he walked away without saying a word.

I watched him until he made it to the hostess stand. Nothing was going right.

"Well, that went more smoothly than I anticipated. I expected him to put up more of a fight." Dad picked up his fork. "Food looks great. Where did you hear about this place?"

Mom wiped her eyes and met my gaze across the table. "Cami posted about it on that picture app."

If Mom knew about this place from what I'd posted, she also knew I was in love. I hadn't made a secret of that. Neither had Harper moments ago.

The raw apology in her expression told me that she knew.

My dad had completely embarrassed me, and Harper had left. Those were two separate problems, and I'd have to deal with them one at a time.

I gripped my napkin in my joined hands as I stood up because I didn't want my dad to see me shaking. "I have tried to walk a tightrope between living in a way that makes me happy and being the daughter you've always wanted. But that isn't working." My emotions were in knots, but my thoughts were clear and unfiltered. "You don't know the first thing about love. You love the idea of having a daughter. But you don't love *me*. When I stopped asking for money, you stopped acting like you cared. That's not how *love* works." I pointed across the restaurant in the direction Harper had gone. "I love that man. And he loves me… not because I'm great at my job or because I'm beautiful. There is no *because*. He just loves me." I laid my napkin on the table. "Mom, you have my address if you ever need to contact me. And if I move, you can ask Joji about me. She'll always know how to find me."

That last part probably stabbed at Mom's heart, but the words were true. Joji had become my family.

My rant might not have made sense to them. But for me, it cauterized a wound.

Dad motioned for me to sit down. "What's the point in making a display? He left you. Walked away without even saying goodbye." His tone was icy and cruel.

I took one step away from the table, struggling to choke out a goodbye without screaming at my heartless father. Part of me didn't want to believe that Harper had left, but could I blame him if he had?

Mom started crying, which she never did in public. "Where are you going?"

"I'm walking home."

"You can't. Someone might grab you off that dark road." She sobbed between words.

"I'll take my chances." I waved over my shoulder, avoiding eye contact with the other restaurant patrons as I marched toward the door.

Tunnel vision set in as I walked through the dining room. Staring at the door handles, I made that my goal. Once outside, I'd figure out how to get home.

When I reached the hostess station, the woman who had seated us motioned for me to stop. "Ma'am."

I shook my head and kept walking. After the scene I'd just made, I needed air and space. I couldn't stop to talk.

Cold air slapped me in the face as I opened the door. I wrapped my arms around myself and scanned the parking lot. I didn't see Harper.

My hope that he'd be waiting outside shattered.

I marched toward the road. My next focus was getting home.

The longest part of the walk was the driveway leading to the road. Why when I was trying to make a statement by walking away did I have to choose places with obnoxiously long driveways? And in heels.

Wiping tears as I walked, I tried to reassure myself that

things with Harper would be okay. Would he blame me for how my father talked to him?

Maybe Harper was waiting for me at the trailer. Or maybe he really had left. He knew how much my parents' approval meant to me.

But that had changed. I had changed.

Footsteps sounded behind me, and either Mom was about to be right, or my father was chasing after me. I didn't want to deal with either possibility, so I hurried my pace, which wasn't exactly easy in heels.

The footsteps drew closer. "What about your tail?" Behind me the sweetest voice in the world rang out loud and clear.

I spun around and bolted toward Harper, praying I wouldn't turn an ankle. As I threw my arms around his neck, he lifted me off the ground, sending my heels flying.

"You didn't leave."

"Of course I didn't leave. I paced in the men's room until I was sure I wouldn't embarrass you, then I walked back to the table."

"Oh no!" Visions of a fist fight played in my head.

"Your mom caught my eye before I made it all the way there. She pointed at the door. I apologized to the hostess about the drama, and she told me you were walking home."

My trust in Harper hadn't been misplaced.

"I'm sorry I ever left the table, but I promised you I would be on my best behavior, and to keep that promise, I walked away. I'm so sorry about making a scene." He kissed the top of my head.

Shivering, I cried into his shoulder. "You didn't make a scene, but I sure did."

He rubbed my back. "You're freezing. Let's get you home."

"I have to find my shoes first. I can't just keep leaving stuff every time I hug you in public."

He turned on his phone flashlight, and we spotted my shoes.

After grabbing them, he swept me into his arms. "I'm sorry things didn't work out like you hoped."

"I wish you could've heard what I said to them."

"Not necessary. I can see confidence and relief written all over you. I'm so proud of you."

"That means the world to me. You mean the world to me."

He carried me to the truck. "Your place or mine?"

"My place."

"Good. It's close, and I just want to hold you."

When we parked in front of the trailer, Joji waved from my porch. "I'm guessing there is a story behind this. Jeffrey is on the phone for you."

I took the phone. "I'm so sorry for what happened in your restaurant."

Joji shot a look at Harper. He shook his head and crinkled his nose, letting her know dinner had not gone well.

Jeffrey surprised me with his relaxed manner. "No worries, doll. The hostess told me all about it. I'm sending a guy over with your dinner. Let me know if we didn't get it right."

"Thank you. That's too kind." I choked out the words, trying not to cry.

"Any friend of Joji's is a friend of mine. Have a great evening." He ended the call.

Pointing over my shoulder as if they didn't know where the restaurant was, I said, "The Cowboy Chef is sending over dinner."

"That was the real reason I went anyway." Harper winked. "You know I'm joking."

I handed the phone back to Joji. "I promise to fill you in tomorrow. I'm okay." I pulled Harper closer to me. "Better than okay."

"Love ya, darling." Joji blew a kiss, then walked back to her house.

"I love you too." I knew the real meaning of family now, and I promised myself that I'd never forget.

Before Joji had even made it to her door, a truck pulled in, and a guy jumped out, holding a bag. "Compliments of the chef."

"Thank you so much." Harper shook the man's hand and accepted the food.

We stood on the porch as the man drove away.

Harper rubbed my back. "Let's get out of the cold."

After all the chaos, it was just the two of us.

He carried the bag into the house and set our dinner on the table, then hugged me close. "Are you really okay? I feel horrible that you thought I'd left."

"I was a giant knot of emotions. Surprisingly, I don't feel like my world just exploded. When you walked away, I worried that you'd think I wanted their approval so much that I'd let that get between us."

He shook his head. "Are you kidding? I'm your hero." He rested his forehead against mine. "But the thought crossed my mind."

"I'm done chasing after a dangling carrot. Love isn't supposed to be a carrot."

With his arms tight around me, Harper whispered in my ear. "Boingo might think so."

I laughed so hard I snorted, which wasn't a wise choice after crying.

"That's the best medicine." He kissed my forehead. "Let's eat before it gets cold."

"Your mom asked about us coming up for Thanksgiving, didn't she?"

"She did."

"I'd love to spend the holiday with your family."

Love abounded in Harper's family, and I wanted to soak it all in.

"I'll call her after we eat."

I wouldn't be alone for Thanksgiving. And I had a whole lot to be thankful for.

CHAPTER 25

In the two weeks leading up to Thanksgiving, I was the busiest I'd ever been. Balancing goat farming with admin work at the studio and all my social media stuff took up all my time.

Standing in front of the llamas, I tried getting them to face me. When they were in a stubborn mood, talking to them was a waste of air.

But I wasn't one to give up easily. "Please, guys. Look this way for just a second."

They looked, and just as I snapped a picture, they spat at me. It was nasty, but it made for a great shot.

As I walked back toward the trailer, Harper hopped out of his truck. "Missed you, so I brought dinner."

"You wonderful, sweet man. This week has been extra crazy. I have a few others asking about managing their social media, but I can't because there aren't enough hours in the day for me to do anything more right now." I pointed at my face. "Let me wash off the llama spit; then we can chat."

"Nice, aren't they?"

I hollered down the hall. "They just don't like being told what to do."

That was something I fully understood.

He was setting out barbecue on the table when I walked back into the room. "Have you thought about not answering phones at the studio and using that time to develop your social media business?"

"I don't want to leave Haley and Nacha stranded." I'd thought about it quite a bit, but they'd been so kind to give me a job when I needed it. I didn't want to seem disloyal.

"What can it hurt to talk to them about it?" He pulled plates and flatware out of the cabinets. "You play favorites with your mugs, don't you?"

"Yes. I have two favorites. I use them on alternating days. Why?"

"Because in one of your poor ignored mugs, there is still a note."

"Oh, I found that one, but I leave it there because I like waking up to you calling me gorgeous." I grabbed drinks. "What time are we leaving tomorrow? Joji said she had everything covered, and I'm sure Clint will be here to help her."

"Let's plan on leaving about seven if that's not too early."

"That works. I finished scheduling all my posts, so I'm all yours."

"Words I love to hear."

I piled brisket on my plate. "Mom called me today. I let it roll to voicemail because I wasn't sure what she'd say. But she left a message."

"And?"

"She was checking to make sure I had somewhere to go for Thanksgiving." I stabbed at my food. "I think she feels trapped between doing what my dad wants and wanting to be my mom."

"I feel for her, but that's a choice only she can make."

"Yep, and I'm not trying to pull them apart. That was never my intent."

"I think she knows that, Cami. Maybe you should call her back after dinner."

"Good idea." I patted his hand. "Thanks for coming tonight."

He grinned. "You all packed?"

"Even my boots. I've never been to a themed taco night."

"My mom likes to make things fun." He picked up his phone and took a picture of me. "Just like someone else I know."

I blew him a kiss.

After dinner, while Harper washed the few dishes, I texted my mom. *Is now an okay time to call?*

Her response made me sad. *Tomorrow would be better. But I hate the thought of you alone. Will Harper be with you?*

He will be. I left off the part about spending the holiday with his family.

Mom didn't need to hear that right now.

***

Leaving early was the right decision. Because we only made one brief stop, we arrived at his parents' house in time for lunch.

The house was quiet. Only his parents were there.

Mel hugged me. "I'd never been one for all those pictures on social media, but now, I just can't get enough. Evan says I'm on there too much. But you post such fun stuff. That venue looks incredible."

"It is. The pictures don't even fully capture how pretty it is out there."

She motioned for me to follow her down the hall. "If

you'd feel more comfortable in a separate room, I can shuffle people around. We'll figure out how to make it work."

"I don't mind sharing the room with Harper, I mean Ethan. And I don't mind Chap staying in there either. You've raised a gentleman, but Chap keeps him in line."

She patted my cheek. "I couldn't have picked anyone more perfect for my son. And I have no problem with you calling him Harper."

"Okay, good to know. And I love your son more than I know how to say."

"I can tell that from the way you look at him. Like he's a superhero or something."

"He's *my* superhero."

"I always do a themed taco bar the night before Thanksgiving. I hope Ethan mentioned that. This year, it's cowboy themed. Easy to serve and easy to clean up. And adding a theme makes it extra fun." She winked. "If you didn't bring anything, we'll get you something to wear."

"He mentioned it. I came prepared." I knew those red bandanas would prove useful.

* * *

IT WAS ENTIRELY possible that I was more excited about seeing Harper in a cowboy hat tonight than I was about eating turkey tomorrow. And I loved Thanksgiving dinner.

I tied the bandana like a headband, making sure the ends were poofed just right. My fitted jeans and new boots were perfect for the theme.

Once I was ready, I wandered out to the kitchen. "Anything I can do to help?"

Mel shook her head. "I think everything is ready. I'm just waiting for everyone to show up."

ONE CHOICE I'D NEVER MAKE

"Have you seen Harper? I wanted a sneak peek at his outfit."

She waved her hand as she turned toward the stove. "He's around."

Within minutes, all his sisters and their families were milling around the large kitchen and dining room. One person was missing.

Evan whistled, and everyone quieted. "Tomorrow, we'll do our tradition of going around the table and saying one thing we're thankful for, but tonight, I'm thankful that we have one more person at our table. Cami, we couldn't be more pleased to have you."

"Thank you." I wiped my eyes.

All this loving family stuff was going to mess up my makeup.

Emmy snorted whatever it was she'd just sipped. Then her sisters started laughing.

I scanned the room and quickly saw why.

Shirtless, but wearing a cowboy hat, Harper strolled toward me. "I requested the theme."

"Because of the hat."

"Because of this." He dropped to one knee and pulled a small velvet box out of his pocket.

I covered my mouth. There was no hope for my makeup.

"Cami, you've lassoed my heart. Will you rescue me from a life of loneliness? Will you marry me?"

"Ethan Harper, you know my answer."

"I'd like to hear you say it." He pointed at the phone his mom was holding. "And all our friends at home are waiting to hear you say it."

Home. I smiled at the camera, then shouted, "Yes. I will marry you, Harper the hero."

The room erupted in cheers. Even Chap joined in on the

ruckus. And I knew there were several people in and near Stadtburg toasting my happiness.

Harper tugged me into the living room and slipped the ring on my finger. "I want to be your family." He wiped a tear off my cheek. "I don't think I've told you about the running joke I've had with my friend Adam. When he proposed to Eve, she called him her superhero. I asked where I could find someone who would call me that. And we've joked about that for a year. Then one day, out of the blue, you captured my interest by running up and calling me a hero. And when I saw you at the pool party, do you remember what you called me?"

"My hero." That moment was forever etched in my memory.

"From that moment, I wanted you to be the one. And it was only a short time before I knew you were."

"I don't know if I would've survived these past few months without you."

He kissed my hand. "You would have. But I'm glad I was able to be there for you. I think it's made a stronger *us*."

"It has."

While the rest of his family served themselves tacos, Harper and I expressed our delight about the engagement with our lips. But we weren't talking.

We saved talking for later… when Chap was on the job.

* * *

CHAP CARRIED his treat onto the bed and wriggled his way in between us.

Harper laughed and grabbed my hand. "I think moving him is pointless. He'll be back up here as soon as I get him down."

"He's fine." I rolled onto my side. "What about Eli?"

"What about him?"

"Where will he live?"

"Not with us. I mentioned to him that Joji might have a trailer for rent relatively soon." He chuckled. "Eli will be fine."

"I can't believe how many texts I fielded tonight." I rested my cheek on his hand. "Aren't you worried that someone might recognize you on the cover?"

"Even if that happens, it's totally worth seeing that smile on your face."

I kissed his hand, and Chap looked up from his treat for a second. "I'd have been smiling no matter what when you asked me that question."

"I wasn't going to take any chances." He winked. "Besides, I saw the way you looked at that cover."

"For Halloween, you and I are totally going as book covers." I giggled at the look that crossed his face.

"Tandy won't be invited, will she?"

I ended the laughter with a single question. "Would you be upset if I didn't tell my parents?"

"Not a bit. Whatever you choose to do, I'll support that."

"It's weird because I want them to know, but I don't want to tell them." I scratched Chap's head. "Do you think we should get a dog?"

"If we do, he'll never sleep on our bed. Ever."

"Be careful when you say never. I said I'd never talk to my dad the way I did."

He leaned over Chap and kissed me. "Maybe we'll get a cat. They don't take up nearly as much room."

"What about March or April?"

"We could get a cat then. Is that a good season for cats?" His green eyes twinkled.

"I could ask Lilith what days are open at the venue. I've managed to save a little since I've been doing all this extra stuff. And if we schedule the wedding on maybe a Thursday or a Friday, we might be able to save a little on the venue."

"Cami, don't worry about that right now. I have some money. We'll figure it out."

"I'm sorry. I know typically the bride's parents pay for the wedding, but…"

"I'm not asking your dad for a single dime. And notice that I didn't use the word never." The intensity in his green eyes warmed me through and through.

"I love you." I knew I'd be saying that a lot.

"Good. I have something to say tomorrow when it's my turn to be thankful."

I had so many reasons to be thankful. It would be hard to pick just one.

* * *

THE NEXT DAY, when his family was seated at the table and all eyes focused on me, I turned to face Harper. "I'm thankful for someone who loves me for me and not for who I could be."

Gratitude spilled down my cheeks.

I couldn't wait to marry Ethan Harper.

CHAPTER 26

Leaning against the counter in Joji's kitchen, I spun the ring on my finger. "I need to stop playing with this ring if I'm going to take pictures of you making cheese."

She laughed. "It takes a few days to get used to." Winking, she wiggled her ring finger. "And I still play with mine. Have a seat. I have leftover chocolate cake. Cheesemaking can wait."

I carried the cake to the table while she made coffee. "I've pinched myself several times. This is real."

I knew that of all people, Joji understood. The engagement ring on her finger and the smile on her face were proof of that.

"How did you keep it a secret? I'm guessing you knew before we even left town." I sat down.

"I knew, but I wouldn't have spoiled that surprise. Not for anything." She set sugar and creamer on the table. "Have y'all set a date? I know it's only been a few days, but you did have a five-hour drive."

"No date yet. We're going to work on a budget, and I'm going to ask Lilith about what days are open at the venue. Getting married there is a must. That's where he told me he loved me for the first time."

Joji grabbed my hand as she dropped into a chair. "I would never dream of trying to replace anyone in your life. Having said that, I want you to hear me out. I may be small, but there is plenty of me to go around. I have a niece and nephew who I love to pieces. You are also part of my family. I'm not sure if you knew what you were signing up for when you took the job." She let go of my hand and nudged my cup toward me. "I want to pay for the wedding."

I started shaking my head before I even opened my mouth. "You can't."

She raised one eyebrow. "Can't? Have you been checking my bank statements? I assure you I can."

"That's not what I meant. I mean, it's too much." Accepting this kind of help seemed like the complete opposite of growing up.

"Who else am I going to spend my money on? Goats?"

"Clint."

She laughed. "He doesn't want me for my money."

"Forget I mentioned it. I don't want to hear any more." I covered my ears.

Her laughter continued. "Cami, please let me do this. I want to."

"I don't know."

"Being an adult doesn't mean you do everything yourself."

I sipped my coffee, forgetting that I hadn't added anything to it. My face puckered. "Is there a thought bubble hovering above my head? How did you know to say that?"

"I guessed. Will you at least talk to Harper about it?" She handed me the sugar.

"I'll do that." I almost couldn't wait until he came over to talk about it.

"Good. Now let me grab my stack of wedding magazines. We can peruse them while we enjoy cake."

Bones followed her down the hall. That dog loved her. And it was easy to see why. She was lovable.

When she tossed the beautiful magazines onto the table, I made a decision. I took a picture of the stack, making sure at least one of the titles was visible, then posted the picture without a caption.

Soon Mom would know my news. But I hadn't actually told her. Not really.

After more than an hour of *oohing* and *aahing* over dresses and indulging in cake, Joji cleaned up the table. "You need to run. You have to be at the studio soon."

"I can come back after work to help you make cheese."

She shook her head. "Clint and I have dinner plans. Tomorrow maybe. Will you see Harper tonight?"

"He's coming over and making me dinner. With all the recipes his brother-in-law sent us, Harper is becoming quite the chef. And I'm learning too." I took a picture of the stack of empty containers waiting to be filled with cheese. "I love when he comes over to cook with me."

"Enjoy your evening." She hugged me. "And please think about what I said."

"I will. I promise."

As I hurried out to the truck, I posted the picture and added a caption about new cheese coming soon. Social media engagement leading up to the weekend market was way up after posting a few pictures. We needed to make lots of cheese tomorrow.

While driving to the studio, I thought through ideas for Lilith's venue. The pictures from my picnic with Harper garnered numerous interactions. They spotlighted the beauty of the place. I needed to check the calendar to see when the next event was. Pictures of a party would be great in the feed.

I ran into the studio right on time. "I'm here. Anything new?"

Haley poked her head out of her office. "The owner from the barbecue place stopped in. He was looking for you."

"For me?"

"He said he'd been talking to that Cowboy Chef guy and wanted to chat with you about internet stuff." Her grin widened as she talked. "You're famous in this town, Cami."

Not wanting to be disloyal, I sorted through words, trying to form a well-structured sentence. Opportunity was knocking at my door, and I couldn't ignore it. "What is the possibility that I could drop back to maybe two or three days a week? I don't want to leave you and Nacha in a lurch."

"We can manage that. Nacha isn't out of the office much these days, and I know she doesn't mind answering the phone. I'm glad you brought it up. You're good at the social media stuff. And you don't need to continue answering phones out of a sense of loyalty. When you need to quit altogether, let us know." She sipped her coffee, looking at me over the rim.

"Thank you. I will keep you posted." I turned on my computer.

"And in the meantime, you'll only answer the phone. We can deal with the other admin duties."

"Are you sure?"

"Yes, and we need to figure out an agreement for you as our social media manager. You've been doing that as a bonus. It's time we worked up a contract for your services." She tossed her empty cup in the trash.

Before I could jump up and down, thanking her, the

phone rang. For the better part of the next three hours, I fielded calls, posting and planning whenever I had a few quiet minutes.

I'd found something I loved doing, and I was good at it. It was almost too good to be true.

* * *

Harper set grocery bags on the counter. "You can work on stuff while I cook."

I hopped onto the counter. "Thanks. Did you have a good day?"

"Pretty good. You're in a chipper mood. I'm guessing that means your day was also good?"

I tugged him close. "You were right."

One eyebrow lifted as a smile spread across his face. "I'm going to like this conversation, I think."

"I talked to Haley about cutting back my work hours. For now, I'm rolling back to three days, but that may change to two. And I'm meeting with the guy from the barbecue place tomorrow."

He pulled me to his lips. "I'm proud of you. And so happy that people see how talented you are."

I leaned my forehead against his. "I want your opinion on something."

He cocked his head without pulling away. "You look amazing in the leopard suit, but I think a dress of some sort might be better for the wedding."

"If money wasn't an issue, when would you want to get married?"

His shoulders tensed. "Cami, I'd marry you tomorrow, but letting your dad have any part in this is a risk. I'm not sure it's worth it."

"Joji wants to pay for everything. She made me promise

I'd talk to you about it." I inhaled, trying to shed the guilt I associated with accepting the money. "At first I was set against it, but I keep thinking about how amazing it would be to be Mrs. Harper at Christmas. Am I crazy?"

That brilliant twinkle danced in his green eyes. "Less than a month? That's the best thing I've heard since you said yes. And while I understand that accepting her offer is uncomfortable, I think being able to give that to you means something to her."

"So it's not selfish to accept it?"

"No, Cami, it's not. And it isn't like you are going to throw a million-dollar event."

"Oh my gosh, no." I giggled as he pulled me off the counter and into his arms.

He carried me to the sofa. "Dinner can wait a few minutes. We have a wedding to plan. Well, you do. I'm just here to do whatever you tell me. What about working on the goat farm?"

"I'll talk to her about that. If she needs my help, I can drive out and do stuff. But being here was a temporary thing."

"Then you'll have more time to grow your business."

"If that's okay." Excitement flared in my chest.

"Totally."

I patted those fireman muscles. "While you're cooking, I'll let Joji know, and I'll send Lilith a note about dates in December. The chapel will look beautiful with greenery."

"And mistletoe." Harper rubbed my back. "I know the next few weeks will be crazy. So, please ask if there is anything I can do."

"Oh, I'm sure you'll have a honey-do list a mile long." I kissed his cheek before climbing out of his lap. "Let's start cooking. I'm starved."

"I'll start. You go talk to Joji."

"Okay. Be right back." Walking to her house, I thought of my mom. Inviting my parents to the wedding felt like a risk my heart couldn't take. Even after everything that happened, I wanted them there for my big day, but having my heart smashed again would hurt too much.

I knocked. Because when Clint's truck was outside, I never walked in without notice. Joji had said he came over to watch movies and television. But as a teen, I'd learned what euphemisms were. My mom would say that she and my dad were going to watch television, but I guess they didn't realize I could hear when their television was on. And when it wasn't.

Shaking that memory, I smiled as the door opened.

Clint grinned. "Evening. Joji's in the kitchen."

Driven by an impulse I couldn't name, I hugged him. "Thanks."

He held me a second longer than I'd expected. "I'm excited for you, Cami." Stepping back, he shoved his hands in his pockets. "And if there is any way I can help you, let me know. Joji's family is my family."

Maybe that was his way of offering to walk me down the aisle. I had to think about it longer before deciding. But no matter what he meant, I appreciated his approval.

I'd been trying to reshape my life to win my parents approval, making choices that fit me. I'd learned that I thrived off approval, but finding it in the right places was key.

Joji walked to the door. "Did you talk to Harper?"

"Yes, and we'd love to accept your generous offer." Before I finished speaking, I threw my arms around her. "We want to get married before Christmas if possible."

"Fun! That's perfect." She shooed me toward the door.

"We'll talk more tomorrow, but tonight, spend time with Harper."

"He'll need it. Wedding planning isn't for the faint of heart." Clint winked.

The next few weeks would be a whirlwind, but at the end, I'd be having the best Christmas ever.

CHAPTER 27

HARPER

Parked along the curb in the posh Houston-area neighborhood, I stood out like a sore thumb. Hopefully, the police wouldn't show up. That was a wrinkle I didn't need.

Putting a smile on Cami's face was the reason I'd traveled three hours, but this mission had to be done in two parts.

When the Maserati pulled out of the driveway, I waited until it was down the street and around the corner before pulling up to Cami's house.

I knocked at the front door and adjusted my collar. I shouldn't be nervous. It didn't matter to me what her parents said. I was here to invite them to the wedding. If they declined the invitation, I'd take that secret to my grave.

If they showed up to the wedding, my bride's smile would be extra bright. And I'd do almost anything to make that happen.

The door opened, and Mrs. Phillips gasped. "Is Cami here?" She stepped outside and looked toward the truck. "Is she okay?"

The concern in her voice gave me hope that perhaps she felt differently than her husband.

"Cami's fine. She's not with me. In fact, she doesn't know I'm here."

She stepped aside and opened the door all the way. "Would you like to come in?"

"Thank you." I followed her through the grand entryway into a sunlit room.

She pointed at a chair as she sat in another. Tears brimmed in her eyes. "When is the wedding?"

This would be easier without the small talk.

"In a week."

"So soon?" A tear streaked down her cheek. "I've been seeing her pictures. She seems happy."

"She is, but she misses you."

"What brings you here? If there is anything I can do…"

I held out the embossed invitation. "I wanted to invite you in person. Having you there would mean the world to Cami."

She trailed a finger over the card. "You drove all this way to invite us?"

"If you decide not to go, Cami will never know." My tone was kind, but I didn't filter the raw truth.

"I know how it looks, but I do love her." Her composure was cracking.

I nodded.

She wiped her eyes and let out a breath. "How long will you be in town?"

"I have one more errand to run; then I'll head back to Stadtburg."

"Will you stop by here before you leave?" She clasped my hand. "Please."

"Of course. Give me about an hour." I stood.

Mrs. Phillips hugged me. "Thank you. You'll never know what this means to me."

"Thank you for not slamming the door in my face."

She patted my arm. "You love her. That's what matters to me."

"I do love her. That's why I came."

Her smile returned. "I'll see you soon."

After a quick wave, I climbed into the truck. The first part of my mission had gone well. I still didn't know if Cami's mom would show up to the wedding, but I hadn't been slapped or had the door closed in my face.

I wasn't as sure one of those wouldn't happen during this second part. I doubted Mr. Phillips would slap me. Getting slugged was more of a possibility.

When I parked outside the office building, I checked my phone for messages before walking inside. Cami hadn't asked many questions about why I couldn't do the cake tasting with her, and I prayed she wasn't suspicious about my absence.

The lobby was spacious and open with light pouring in all the windows. I walked up to the front desk, and a young woman smiled. "How may I help you?"

"I'm here to see Mr. Phillips."

Her brow furrowed as she typed on a computer. "What name should I give? Do you have an appointment?"

"My name is Ethan Harper. And I don't have an appointment. You can tell him it relates to his daughter."

Shock registered on the woman's face, but she recovered quickly. "Give me a second, and I'll see if he's available."

I moved away from the desk, giving her space to make the uncomfortable call.

Would I be sent away? Called into his office? Or would he simply rush down the grand staircase and slug me in the lobby?

The curiosity was eating at me.

A minute later, Cami's father appeared at the top of the stairs. "I'll see you now."

Taking the stairs two at a time, I made it to the top quickly. "Thank you for seeing me. I won't take up much of your time."

"At least we agree on that." He walked down the hall.

I followed.

His assistant stared as I strode through the office. I could only hope that the sweat circles under my armpits weren't visible.

Mr. Phillips closed the door with a little too much force, then dropped into his chair. "Why are you here?"

I'd rehearsed what to say during the drive to Houston, but my brain still felt like it was a cat trying to get traction on a tile floor. "I love your daughter, and despite the way you've treated her, she loves you. And because she does, having you at her wedding would put a smile on her face. That's why I'm here."

His jaw clenched.

But I continued my monologue. "In one week, she's going to walk down the aisle and become my wife. I'm requesting that you attend the wedding."

He shifted as if stabbed by the news of the wedding date. "Are you here asking me to pay for it? Or did you just come to grovel for my blessing?"

Focusing my thoughts on Cami, I forced myself not to react in anger. "I don't need your blessing, and I'm not asking for your money." I scrubbed my face. "I'm just asking you to show your daughter that you love her. *Please.*"

Anger colored his face. "You can leave now."

"Thank you for your time. Also, she doesn't know I came here. As much as she'd love to have you there, she was afraid you wouldn't come if she asked. I was trying to save her that rejection." I dropped the invitation onto his desk. "If you love her, you won't rub her nose in that rejection."

I slipped out of the office, avoiding the stare from the assistant.

That had gone about as well as expected.

I had time to kill before showing up at Cami's house again. Why hadn't I asked why her mom wanted me to stop by again? All I wanted to do now was race home to Cami.

Sitting in a coffee shop, I texted her. *I hope your day is going well.*

It is. Busy but good. I'm tasting cake later at Tessa's. Since you're busy, Eli volunteered to give me a guy's perspective. Her reply gave no hint of suspicion about what I was really doing.

I responded right away. *With cake involved, why am I not surprised? Love you. I'll message again when I'm finished.*

Love you too. She chased her last text with a heart.

After coffee, I drove back to the house.

A pile of luggage on the porch surprised me. Was Mrs. Phillips sending Cami's stuff back?

The door opened, and Mrs. Phillips set another bag on top of the pile. "Oh! You're here. I didn't mean to pack so much. I'm sure Cami needs help, and I want to be there. Will you take me to a hotel close to Stadtburg?"

I imagined Cami's face at the moment she saw her mom. "Absolutely. Cami has an extra bedroom. I'm sure she'd love to have you."

"Wonderful. Thank you. I've started to call her so many times. I just wasn't sure she wanted to talk to me."

"She misses you." I picked up two of the bags. "Let me load these, then we can be on our way, Mrs. Phillips."

"Perfect. Please call me Nora. Once we leave, I need to text David and let him know I'll be gone a week." She rubbed her temples. "He won't be pleased."

I loaded all her luggage, then opened the passenger-side door. "I'm ready whenever you are."

"On the way back, I'll tell you all the stories I can remember about Camille. Cami. She is named after her grandmother, her father's mother. That Camille gave life to a room. She broke conventions and could make people laugh with a look." Mrs. Phillips buckled her seat belt. "I can think of so many stories. This will be fun."

My drive home wasn't going to be at all what I expected when I left Mr. Phillip's office. Spending three hours on the road with my future mother-in-law hadn't even been a blip on my radar.

At least I'd been partially successful.

CHAPTER 28

After two weeks of nonstop preparing, I dropped into a chair, sighing as Tessa locked the door. "One more week. After this tasting, I want to fast forward time. There is still a lot to do, but I am so ready to walk down that aisle."

"I have a fresh pot of coffee brewing. Think of this like a spa appointment, only with cake." Tessa set the carafe in the machine.

"Thank you so much for this. You know I would have been happy with anything you made." I was looking forward to a low-key visit with friends.

Delaney laughed. "Tessa must give options. Is Harper coming? He gets a vote, right?"

"Of course he gets a vote, but he had something he had to do. Eli is coming to give a guy's opinion."

Tessa set a tray of small cakes on the table. "That must be who is knocking at the back door. Let me grab it."

Before Eli appeared, I touched Delaney's hand. "That's who I'm going to have you walk out with. You know him, right?"

"Funny thing, I don't. I've seen him around, but we've never met."

"Well, if you hate him, let me know. I can switch up the order or something." I flashed a smile as Eli came into view. "Hiya, thanks for being willing to give up an hour eating cake."

That wide Gallagher grin spread across his face. "Sacrifices must be made." Then his gaze shifted to Delaney, and he froze.

That change in behavior was interesting. And all I could think about was what Harper had said.

"Eli, have you met Delaney?" I couldn't wait to tell Harper about the way Eli was reacting.

Eli shook his head and extended his hand. The most telling thing was what he didn't do. He didn't say a word.

After shaking his hand, Delaney pulled out the chair next to her. "Nice to meet you. Have a seat."

He dropped into the chair, as stiff as one of my dad's cocktails.

This was going to be fun.

I counted Joji and Clint getting together as a win. Maybe I could add to that list. I could visualize my business cards. Social Media Manager & Matchmaker.

Connection was what the two things had in common.

Tessa set a tray of small cakes on the table. "White with lemon filling. This one has raspberry filling. This is the traditional German chocolate. And this one is a double chocolate. Last one is a red velvet. You need to choose two."

My mouth watered. "I'm not even sure where to start. Everything looks amazing." Angling my camera, I captured a picture of the tray. "This is too yummy not to post."

"Let me grab the coffee. Eli, help me, will you?"

He shot across the room like a clown launched out of a cannon. "Yep."

ONE CHOICE I'D NEVER MAKE

Once we all had coffee and Eli was back in his chair, looking wholly uncomfortable, Tessa cut the first cake into pieces. "Round one."

I forced myself not to devour the entire slice. "This is like a lemon-filled cloud. Oh my word, it's good. I think I could live on this."

Laughing, she cut into the next cake. "Sip the coffee, then we'll taste the next one."

Working our way around the platter, Delaney, Tessa, and I chatted about the different flavors. I knew which cake I wanted for the wedding cake, but getting Eli's input on the groom's cake seemed like the fair thing to do. Besides, it would force him to speak.

"Eli, you've been quiet. What do you think? Would Harper prefer the traditional or one of the others?"

He shrugged. "They're all good."

"Well, do you prefer the almost sensual richness of the double chocolate or the vivid energy of the red velvet?" I nudged his leg with my shoe.

His eyes narrowed, and his normally humorous gaze was filled with icy daggers.

"I need to know what a hero-type guy would want." Watching him squirm spurred me on, and I just kept at it. "Need to taste them again?"

"Double chocolate." He'd worked up to five words, but the deep breath he pulled in warned me not to push him.

"Got it. Sensual chocolate. We'll go with that. And lemon for the wedding cake. I've never tasted anything so delicious." I checked my phone.

There was no message from Harper, but there was a like on my photo. Mom. My stomach knotted.

In the middle of my excitement, there was a sliver of bitterness. But like when I was sick and needed to take medicine, I swallowed the bitter taste and focused on the happy things.

Where was Harper? It had been hours since I'd heard from him. I knew he was busy, but rarely was he out of contact. And right now, I wanted to be wrapped in his arms.

The ready-to-run Eli probably knew where Harper was, and catching Eli off guard was the best way to get an honest answer.

I leaned forward like I was about to share a secret. Delaney and Tessa followed my lead. With Delaney inches from Eli's arm, he stared at the gap like it might implode at any moment.

"I don't know where Harper is." I let loose a dramatic sigh. "He wouldn't say what he was doing today."

Eli rolled his eyes. "He's almost to your place."

"Really? He hasn't called." I crossed my arms. "I figured you'd know."

"You could've just asked." He glanced at Delaney, then sprang out of his chair. "If you don't need me anymore, I'm going to go."

"I'll walk you out." Tessa picked up the tray.

I snagged the last of my favorite cake. "I'll just take this. And thanks, Eli."

Delaney watched as he strode toward the back. "Quiet, isn't he?"

"Not always." I wasn't ready to tell her what that meant, but I couldn't wait to talk to Harper about it.

By the time Tessa made it back to the table, I'd shoveled an entire piece of cake into my mouth.

She refilled our coffee cups. "He was in a mood."

"We can talk about him later. And believe me, I want to, but right now, we have other issues." Delaney pointed at my plate. "What's wrong, Cami? I haven't seen you down food like that since when you ate all that ice cream when you were drowning your sorrows over leaving Harper on the sidewalk."

I loved having friends, but having them know me so well made avoiding some conversations impossible. "Mom liked the picture of the cakes. I feel bad that I haven't invited them. I'd be thrilled if they showed up, but if I asked and they didn't come, I'd eat the entire wedding cake without sharing. And I should at least share with Harper. You know, for pictures."

Tessa hugged me. "I'm sorry. It's not too late to ask Clint to walk you down the aisle. Then you might not feel as alone."

I wadded a napkin into my fist. "Thanks to all of you, I don't feel alone at all. Really."

"And you aren't upset about Harper being MIA?" Delaney sipped her coffee.

"No. I've missed seeing him today, but it's not like he's off doing something awful. I trust him." I savored the robust coffee. "But as soon as I finish this, I'm racing home to see him."

"Knowing Harper, he probably went to a nursery and picked you an entire bouquet with his own hands." Delaney laughed. "He's a bit of a romantic when it comes to you."

"All that is just icing on the cake." I slapped the table. "Now before I go, any objection to walking out with Eli?"

Delaney shook her head. "No objections. He's a cutie. I just won't plan on conversation."

"If he doesn't talk to you, it means—" Tessa yelped when I kicked her shin. "What?"

"Sorry. He's weird. Don't let him bother you." I picked up my purse. "I'm not sure I know how to thank the two of you properly. Walking into this doughnut shop has made my life so much better."

"Maybe that should be written on the door." Tessa grinned. "And we love you too."

After a group hug, I raced out to the truck, eager to see Harper. Before backing out of the parking space, I called him.

The call rang once before going to voicemail.

Instead of panicking, I shot off a text. *On my way home. Will you be over later?*

A kissing emoji popped up as an answer.

Something was up, but I didn't have the first clue what it might be.

THE ANSWER to my text waited for me at the farm. Harper's truck was parked outside the trailer, and he stood on my porch.

"Hello, gorgeous." He met me at the bottom stair. "I have a surprise for you."

That statement wasn't completely unexpected. He'd been gone all day doing something, and this close to the wedding, I guessed it somehow related to me.

I wrapped my arms around him. "Do you?"

After a lingering kiss, he swung me around. "How was the tasting?"

"Tessa is amazing. I chose double chocolate for the groom's cake and lemon-filled for the tiered cake. Oh, and Eli showed up and maybe said ten words."

Harper cocked his head. "With you and Tessa?"

"And Delaney." I poked him in the chest. "You know what that means, don't you?"

Chuckling, he shook his head. "Can you at least wait until after the wedding to play matchmaker?"

"Believe me, marrying you is my priority."

"Good." He clasped my hand. "The surprise is at Joji's."

"Joji is right there." I waved as she walked into the barn.

"Inside her house. Let's go." He tugged me toward her porch. "You'll want to see this."

I pushed open the door and was met with a scream.

My beautiful, poised mother was up on the counter on her hands and knees. "Help me." She pointed at the ground where Joji's smallest kitten wiggled his rump as if ready to jump.

Caught between the urge to laugh and the need to cry, I scooped up the kitten. "Mom."

"Put him outside. Please." Panic etched on my mom's face in all the places wrinkles were supposed to be. Her plastic surgeon was a skilled man.

I handed the kitten off to Harper. "You did this, didn't you?"

He set the cat on the front porch. "Your mom? Yes. I didn't have anything to do with the cat. I had no idea she didn't like them."

"Phobia." I put my hand out to help her down. "I'm so happy to see you."

She inched her way to the edge of the counter. "Are there more of them?"

Harper ran down the hall, checking for fuzzy creatures.

"He'll make sure they are all outside." I grabbed her hand. "You can get down."

"How embarrassing. And how did you know I had a phobia?" The bewilderment on her face was welcome after seeing her panic.

"It's a bit obvious." I helped her to the ground.

As soon as her feet hit the floor, she wrapped me in a hug. "Does he make you happy?"

"Very happy." I'd never been so thrilled to see my mom.

"Harper said you have an extra bedroom. If that doesn't work, I'm happy to stay at a hotel."

"You are more than welcome in my extra room."

This would definitely make for an interesting week. Mom would be spending a week in a small trailer, and she'd be on a goat farm. What could go wrong?

With such a happy surprise, I didn't shatter any part of it by asking about my dad. He wasn't here, and that spoke volumes.

CHAPTER 29

*H*arper brushed a thumb on my cheek. "I learned all about your grandmother. Sounds like you are a lot like her."

"She made me feel not crazy. I loved her." I nestled against him and pulled the blanket tighter around us. "Thank you. I'm shocked she came."

"It's clear she loves you. I had to give it a shot."

"It might get a little nuts with her here, but I am happy she came. I'm saying that now before I call you ranting about my mom."

He laughed. "You going to introduce her to the goats?"

"I plan to. I'll just have to chase the cats out of the barn first."

The evening had been a whirlwind. Joji had made dinner, and we'd all talked for hours. But I was thankful for a few quiet minutes alone with my love.

"Joji has been awesome. And I can't even tell you how happy I am that Mom and Joji hit it off. That will make this week much easier. Sorry we have to snuggle outside."

"Okay by me. I should let you go visit with your mom." Thankfully, Harper didn't move.

I listened to the night noises, enjoying being with him. "Did he say anything? Or did you even see him?" Explaining who I meant by *him* didn't seem necessary.

Those strong muscles tightened. "My plan was to invite them quietly, so that if they didn't come, you'd never know. But it didn't go the way I'd expected. When I left, I hadn't planned on three hours in the truck with your mom."

I giggled. "I wish I could've been there."

"She kept glancing over at my speedometer. And she'd squeeze her eyes closed whenever a semi-trailer passed us. But she told story after story about you."

"Uh-oh."

"I learned a ton." He nuzzled my neck, then grew serious. "In answer to your original question, I did talk to him. His dislike for me exceeds his love for you, I think. And I'm sorry about that. And I'm sorry you found out about that part of it."

"I know how far you'll go to make me happy."

"Three hours. That's as far as I'll go." Moonlight reflected in his eyes, highlighting the humor dancing there.

"I love you, too, Harper." I trailed a finger through his whiskers. "What was your plan if the trip hadn't been successful? How did you plan to explain being gone all day?"

He crinkled his nose. "I was going to buy you a kitten."

"We'll have to get Mom past her fear before we add a cat to our family."

"No joke. And I love hearing you say that word."

"Family?"

"We."

* * *

ONE CHOICE I'D NEVER MAKE

JUST BEFORE SIX in the morning, I tiptoed out of the trailer. It was my last week feeding the animals, and I wasn't going to skip out on the fun. Working on the farm had changed me, and I'd forever be grateful to Joji and her menagerie of animals.

"Morning, Boingo." I rubbed his head as he trotted along beside me. "Be nice to my mom, please. She isn't used to being around animals."

I grabbed chicken feed and headed toward the pen, and Boingo stayed right on my heels.

He never went in where the chickens were. I think the red hen scared him. Sometimes she scared me.

"Are you ladies going to miss me?" I gathered eggs from the hen house. "I'll miss most of you."

Once the eggs were safely on Joji's porch, I wandered into the barn to set up the milking machine. I'd grown to love the quiet hours of the morning.

But some days, I did miss my bed.

Once the chores were all finished, I handed off the eggs to Joji before slipping back into the trailer. Coffee and I had a standing morning date.

Mom stood in the kitchen, looking like she'd stepped off the set of a reality cooking show. Eggs were smeared on the counter, and flour dusted the counters and her clothes. But the smile on her face was the brightest I'd seen in years.

"I made us breakfast."

The chances of it tasting good were slim to none. "Perfect. Let me wash up, and I'll make us coffee. I didn't expect you up this early."

"We only have a week. Besides, your father started calling before the sun was up. I didn't exactly tell him where I was headed." She flipped over what was likely supposed to be a pancake.

"You what?"

"I simply sent him a text telling him I'd be home on Sunday. He's a smart man. If he cares to figure it out, he will."

I'd never seen this side of my mom. "Did you answer his phone call?"

"Nope. Just sent a text with a picture of flour and eggs. Told him I was busy making pancakes." She wet a dishrag and wiped her face. "I'm sorry for how he acted and for not taking your side at the restaurant."

"I'm just glad you're here." After she added the last pancake to the stack, I snapped a picture and posted it with a simple caption. *Breakfast with my mom.*

Dad was probably worried about her, but he'd figure out where she was with a little research.

"And Cami, you snagged a good one in Harper. He drives a little bit fast, but he loves you. And *that* is what's important. I miss the days when your father looked at me like Harper looks at you."

"He does love me. And I prefer to think my parents welcomed a stork one day."

Mom laughed. "Oh, no. Once upon a time, your father—"

I covered my ears. "Not listening." Watching her out of the corner of my eye, I laughed at her reaction to my antics.

"You are so much like your grandmother. She'd be so proud of you. I am. Harper told me about the social media business you're building."

"Being a grownup isn't as hard as I thought it might be." I popped a bite of pancake into my mouth, then forced myself to swallow it.

Mom did the same. "Oh my. These are awful. Spit it out. Hurry. You don't need to get sick." She shoved her plate far away from her. "I tried."

"Come into the kitchen. We'll make a new batch together."

"I used all the eggs." Mom pointed at the mess on the counter.

I slipped on my shoes. "I just gathered some this morning. I'll be right back."

"Oh that's right! This is a farm."

Mom and I spent the next hour making pancakes and enjoying them. Something had shifted in the relationship, and I loved how it was. In truth, it wasn't surprising that things were different. I'd changed, and watching the woman in my trailer made it clear that Mom had changed.

I really hoped Mom and Dad would be able to work things out once she went home. Given her new—or maybe rediscovered—spunk, he would likely be getting more than he bargained for.

CHAPTER 30

I woke up to butterflies throwing a rave in my stomach. In six hours, I'd be walking down the aisle. And if I had any hope of being ready, I needed coffee now.

As I walked into the living room, I caught Mom taking a closeup of my dress.

"Please don't post that picture anywhere. I don't want Harper to see it before the doors open at the back of the chapel." The imagined look on his face made my heart beat faster.

"Give me some credit. I wouldn't ruin that man's surprise. You're going to knock him off his feet."

"I just about did the day I met him." I reminded myself that running down the aisle and throwing my arms around him broke all convention. That didn't make it any less tempting. "Coffee?"

"Please. Joji gave me a cup earlier, but I could use another." Mom seemed more relaxed than I'd ever seen her.

"Joji? Were you out when she was feeding the animals?"

She grinned. "I was. Shocking, isn't it?" In the kitchen, she pulled a plate out of the fridge. "She sent breakfast."

"I've enjoyed having you here this week. I'm not sure if I've said that." I would relish the memories made in just a few days. After the last few months, these shared moments were even sweeter.

"Me too." She served the cheese toast onto plates. "Joji is impressive. That she took all this on by herself amazes me. And you're a lot like her."

"No making me cry this morning. That isn't allowed. Delaney will be here to do my makeup in less than an hour, and I don't need puffy eyes." I set two cups of coffee on the table. "I'll be doing my share of crying at the ceremony."

"You and me both. While we eat, let's go over the lists and make sure everything is covered. Are you packed?"

"Yep. And you can stay here as long as you need. Eli said he was fine with that. He'll move in after you go home."

Mom squeezed my hand. "I'm going home right after the wedding. I'm not ready to give up hope that the man I married is buried under all that bluster. But I promise to visit."

"I'll fix up the guest room when we return from the honeymoon."

I pulled the list close and scanned it. "I'm so excited I might pop."

Over breakfast, Mom and I focused on what needed to be done. A busy few hours lay ahead of us.

* * *

BIRDS CHIRPED. The sun was shining on a perfect December day. Christmas was about a week away, and I was getting the best present in the entire world.

Tessa held my bouquet as I maneuvered my way into the motor cart.

Clint winked. "You look amazing, Cami."

"Thanks."

Joji slipped in next to me and grabbed my hand. "Lilith sent this picture."

Harper and his groomsmen were lined up near the altar.

"Would you look at all those good-looking men?" Joji grinned.

"Hey there." Clint gave her a quick kiss. "Hold on tight. Ready, Beau?"

The bridesmaids were in the cart Beau was driving.

"As I'll ever be." Beau seemed to relish his role as chauffeur.

We pulled away from the bridal house and drove through the venue.

Clint parked the motor cart outside the chapel. "Ready or not, the time has come."

"Oh, I'm ready." I gathered my full skirt and stepped out onto the red carpet that had been laid down outside the small white chapel.

Joji climbed out after me.

"Let us help you." Tessa jumped out of the other cart.

Haley, Delaney, and Lilith ran over, shaking their heads.

"Slow down a bit. They'll wait for you, I promise." Joji hugged me. "Harper isn't leaving that altar without you. Guaranteed."

"I know. I know. I'm just excited is all." I was counting the seconds until seeing Harper at the front.

Clint held out his arm to Joji, and they slipped inside.

Music played inside the chapel, and only minutes separated me from married life.

Haley, Tessa, and Delaney lined up, and then one by one they made their way down the aisle.

I stood outside the double doors, waiting for Lilith to give me the signal. I hadn't made the decision to walk in alone lightly.

After all that changed in the last few months, I didn't need anyone giving me away. Harper was my choice, and I'd walk to meet him all alone.

When she nodded at Beau to open the doors, I inhaled.

This was the moment.

Instead of opening the door, he stared over my shoulder. The question in his brow was unmistakable. My dad's car skidded to a stop in a cloud of dust, and then he ran toward me.

I wanted to believe that his suit signaled good news. Would he have dressed up to crash a wedding?

Lilith positioned herself in front of me. "How can I help you?"

"If it's okay with my daughter, I want to watch her get married." The softness in his brown eyes surprised me. But there was regret mixed with it.

Nodding, I willed myself not to cry. "I asked Mom to save a seat for you."

"Your mother sent me a picture of the dress this morning. And she was right. If I'd missed this smile on your face, I would regret it the rest of my life." He stepped closer. "You look beautiful."

"Thank you."

His lips pinched. "I have a lot to apologize for."

I wasn't sure what had prompted this surprising change of heart, but I couldn't handle that conversation right now.

Lilith held up her hand. "Hold that thought. Harper is probably getting nervous. Her music has already played once and just restarted. I don't need him passing out at the front." She nudged my father toward the door. "Hurry."

He kissed my cheek. "Do you want me to walk you down the aisle?"

I shook my head. "I'll walk in alone."

After a quick nod, he slipped inside. Whatever Mom had texted this morning must've had an impact. Or maybe it was something Harper had said to my dad.

My poor Harper was probably a basket case since I hadn't walked up the aisle.

"They aren't brawling, are they?" I itched to peek in the door.

"Perfectly civil. Now smile." Lilith pointed at Beau, and each of them pulled open one of the doors.

Harper's gaze snapped to me, and his shoulders relaxed.

I blew him a kiss before taking the first step.

With my gaze locked with Harper's, I counted in my head like Lilith had instructed. Then, slowly I marched up the aisle.

His smile widened with every one of my steps.

The slow walk lasted until I was only a few steps from my love. I broke into a run and threw my arms around his neck. Flower petals landed near his feet.

The good-looking minister chuckled. "Someone is a wee bit excited."

Harper kissed my forehead. "I am."

Once the laughter died down, Minister Mad Dog Miller —that was what everyone called him—started the ceremony.

"Friends and family, we are gathered here on this beautiful December day to witness the union of Camille Phillips and Ethan Harper."

My mom's sniffles echoed in the small chapel, and even my dad wiped at tears.

The ceremony continued just like I had dreamed over and over during the last few weeks.

And when Harper heard the words "You may kiss the bride," he didn't hesitate. And the rest of the room faded away for a brief second.

I'd married my hero.

EPILOGUE

ELI

CAMI & HARPER'S WEDDING

While the guests were focused on Cami and Harper walking down the aisle, I was trying to keep my heartbeat from skyrocketing. Fainting at a wedding wouldn't help my reputation. I was already a laughingstock.

If I had any clue how to untie my tongue when Delaney was near me, I would. I'd compliment her on how beautiful she looked, ask about her hobbies, and invite her to dinner.

But instead, I reverted to a boy and gave grunts in place of words.

And when Delaney touched me the effect was much worse. That was why I was breathing with intention, hoping the thumping in my chest wasn't so loud she could hear it too.

As she rested a hand on my arm, her perfume wrapped around me. It was both pleasant and suffocating at the same time.

Even with my heart lodged in my throat, I didn't want her to let go.

We walked into the reception hall, and she squeezed my arm. "Beautiful, isn't it?"

I managed a nod, then realized she was talking about the wedding. "Yeah. Nice."

Tessa waved, and Delaney's fingers slipped off my arm as she stepped away.

This was when I wanted to be a fly on the wall. I could watch her, but no one would expect me to talk.

Cami glanced over and flashed me a thumbs-up.

She'd just gotten married. Didn't she have enough to think about without teasing me about Delaney?

I found my seat at the wedding party table. The name card next to mine wasn't a surprise. Delaney. I knew so little about her. And I wanted to know more.

But at this rate, by the end of the day, she'd be convinced I was a moron.

After making it through the meal, I braced for the traditional festivities. There was no way the guys were going to let me hide out in the corner when Harper tossed the garter.

Ladies gathered on the dance floor, and I watched Delaney. She and Tessa nudged each other playfully.

"Everyone ready?" Cami held up her bouquet. And every time she moved it, red petals drifted toward the floor. Smashing the bouquet against Harper's back when she'd jumped into his arms hadn't been good for the flowers.

The crowd cheered even before she turned around. With her back to her friends, Cami tossed the bouquet.

Delaney reached up and snagged the flowers out of the air. Cradling the bouquet, she beamed.

Zach slapped my shoulder. "Wipe your chin and go out there."

"Funny." As if it wasn't bad enough that I behaved this way in front of my friends. Having an older cousin witness it all made it worse. He'd known me a long time.

I marched out to the dance floor, ignoring the stare from Cami.

Once all the bachelors were gathered and waiting, Cami perched on a stool, and Harper reached up under her dress.

When he pulled that silly leopard tail from under her dress, the crowd went nuts.

Harper swung it around in a circle, pointing at us. "Beware. There is a fastener at the end of this thing, so be careful. I don't want to have to call in the paramedics."

Hank waved and draped an arm around Nacha's shoulders. Hopefully, she would make it through the day without giving birth at the reception. But her husband was a paramedic, so he could handle it if she did.

Harper turned around, and I made my way to the back of the cluster. One of the other guys could catch that tail.

When I snuck one more look at Delaney, she waved. And I was entranced. The longer I held her gaze, the more fervently she waved.

Maybe she didn't think I was a complete dufus.

Then that stupid tail whapped me in the eye. And that fastener carried a punch.

Harper raced over. "Are you okay?"

I nodded. "I just need a rug to slide under."

He leaned in close. "I'm going to need that tail back."

After shoving the tail at him, I walked off in search of ice.

I was ready for the day to be over.

* * *

THANK you for reading *One Choice I'd Never Make*! I hope you love Cami and Harper's story. Find out what happens with

Delaney and Eli in *Three Rules I'd Never Break*.

Keep Reading for a BONUS epilogue!

BONUS EPILOGUE

HARPER

MORE THAN A YEAR LATER

Coming home after my shift, I never knew what I'd find. Some days, I would find Cami drinking her fourth cup of coffee with a pen stuck in her messy bun and tapping away on the laptop.

Other times, she would walk out of the bedroom, modeling her latest purchase from the lingerie shop. I really liked those mornings.

Once, she was stretched out on the sofa in that leopard costume. I still smiled when I thought about it.

There were never dull moments with Cami around.

Since today was my birthday, I sort of hoped a birthday suit would be part of my surprise.

On my last birthday, she'd given me a pair of kittens. That added to the excitement in the house. It also meant her parents stayed in a hotel when they came. And I was okay with that.

Wondering what today would hold, I pushed open the front door. "Morning. I'm home."

Cami came rushing down the hall, dressed in her cute little pajamas. She launched into my arms. "Happy birthday."

The cats tore down the hall, wanting to be part of the fun.

"Thank you." I loved that she greeted me with the same fervor as the first time she'd met me... and the second.

"Breakfast is ready," she said between kisses. "I made pancakes."

I carried her into the kitchen. "Smells amazing, and I'm starved."

She wriggled out of my arms. "Sit. Let me get you food."

"I'll happily delay eating for a few minutes of holding you." I slipped my arms around her waist.

She leaned back and kissed my cheek. "I know, but we're on a little bit of a schedule."

"A schedule? Now I'm curious."

I let go of her as she carried the platter of pancakes to the table.

"Would you grab the baked omelets out of the oven, please?"

"New recipe?" I inhaled the aroma, then pulled the muffin pans out of the oven.

"Yep. From your sister." She dropped into her chair. "Eat up. You'll get your present later."

"Are you just going to tease about what's coming up?"

Twinkles danced in her eyes. "I want you to be surprised."

As soon as I finished eating, she whisked my plate away. "Let me run and get dressed super quick."

While she was in the bedroom, I filled the cats' food bowls and gave them fresh water. "What does she have planned? Has she told you?"

The lanky black cats flicked their tails but gave no answer. She'd sworn them to secrecy.

"Okay. I'm ready." She eased up in front of me. "I think you'll like this first part."

"Does that mean I won't like the second part?"

"No, silly. I wouldn't have made it part of your birthday plan if I didn't think you'd like it."

Hand in hand, we walked out to my truck. After helping her in, I slid behind the wheel. "Where to?"

"Lilith's venue. They have an event there later so we can only be there for a little while. That's the reason for the schedule. Mostly."

While I drove, we talked about her parents' upcoming visit.

"Dad has been hinting about the SUV, but if it's okay with you, I'd rather not have it back. I like Joji's truck, and bartering social media stuff for a payment is kind of a steal."

"Agreed." I was happy to see her parents involved in our lives, but I liked the financial independence.

Even when they'd shown up with all the stuff Cami had taken home and handed over the keys to the storage unit, she didn't accept all of it. For one thing, I wasn't sure it would fit in our house.

But she'd been intentional about not crossing back into territory she felt free of. And I admired that.

I punched the code into the box by the gate, then parked near the picnic spot where I'd surprised her more than a year ago. A spot was set up on the ground just like it had been that day when I'd told her I loved her.

She leaned across the cab and kissed my cheek. "I love this place."

"Me too."

When I opened her door, she nudged my shoulder. "Turn around and give me a piggyback ride."

After getting to the blanket, I dropped to my knees, and then we landed in a tangled pile.

"I wish we could lie here for hours together, but we only have about thirty minutes. There are already workers running around. But..." She inhaled and pulled a small gift bag out of the cooler. "Open it."

I yanked the tissue out of the top of the bag and shoved it in the cooler.

Cami stared as I pulled the T-shirt out of the bag. "Read the front."

I unfolded it, then looked from the T-shirt that read *Super Dad* to Cami. "Really?"

"Uh-huh." She rubbed her stomach. "I'm not that far along, but as hungry as I am lately, there is no way I can keep this a secret for long. Our friends will either guess that I'm pregnant or think I have a tape worm."

I stretched out and pulled her on top of me. "I love you."

"Love you too. At least we've had a year as cat parents. Think we'll be okay at this?" Her smile was wide, but hesitation swirled in her eyes.

"Cami, you'll be an amazing mom. And you've had more than cats for training. What about the goats and chickens and llamas?"

She laughed. "I guess parenting is like working on a goat farm. No matter how much you read about it or have someone give advice, it is still basically a crash course where knowledge is earned hands-on."

Cami had never been more right.

"Kiss me. Then we're headed to Haley's house for cake and stuff."

"You've planned a full day." I dropped kisses on her neck as she giggled.

"Partially. Cake and friends. Several hours alone. Then dinner at Jeffrey's restaurant. The Cowboy Chef is big news right now. We're fortunate to get a reservation."

"It's lucky I know someone with connections."

Her breath tickled my ear as she whispered, "I'm the lucky one."

True love made us both feel like we'd hit the jackpot. And now we'd get to share that love with a tiny little person.

A NOTE TO READERS

Thank you for reading! I hope you loved Cami and Harper's story.

Have you read Clint and Joji's story? If not, grab a copy of Enchanted by Joji.

Be sure to check out my website at www.RemiCarrington.com for information about upcoming releases and to find other sweet romances. To get updates in your inbox, subscribe to Remi's News. I also like to send my subscribers bonus and exclusive content.

ALSO BY REMI CARRINGTON

Never Say Never

Three Things I'd Never Do
One Guy I'd Never Date
Two Words I'd Never Say Again
One Choice I'd Never Make
Three Rules I'd Never Break
Two Risks I'd Never Take Again
One Whopper of a Love Story
Christmas Love
Christmas Sparkle
Christmas Surprise

Stargazer Springs Ranch

Fall in love with cowboys and spunky women.

Cowboys of Stargazer Springs

The ranch hands are falling in love.

Bluebonnets & Billionaires series

Lots of money & even more swoon.

* * *

Pamela Humphrey, who writes as Remi Carrington, also releases books under her own name. Visit PhreyPress.com for more information about her books.